GUNFIRE AT
ANTELOPE WELLS

Gunfire At Antelope Wells

by

Doc Adams

Dales Large Print Books
Long Preston, North Yorkshire,
BD23 4ND, England.

British Library Cataloguing in Publication Data.

Adams, Doc
    Gunfire at Antelope Wells.

    A catalogue record of this book is
    available from the British Library

    ISBN   1-84262-154-8 pbk

First published in Great Britain in 1999 by Robert Hale Limited

Published in Large Print 2002 by arrangement with
Robert Hale Limited

Dales Large Print is an imprint of Library Magna Books Ltd.

Printed and bound in Great Britain by
T.J. (International) Ltd., Cornwall, PL28 8RW

ONE

Aaron Hunter rode over the hill and looked down at the little town of Antelope Wells. The thirty or forty weatherbeaten shacks seemed to huddle together against the falling dark and the howling wind. Some of them were empty and abandoned, their doors and shutters swinging wildly. Others were still occupied and showed lights. None of the buildings was bigger, or more brightly lit, than the Castle Saloon.

Hunter shrugged his shoulders inside his heavy coat. Unlike most preachers, he had nothing against saloons. Or drink, for that matter, so long as it was honest liquor and drunk in moderation.

Most western towns got started when someone put up a tent beside the trail and opened a saloon. Cowhands would ride miles to get a drink, even if they knew damn well it was made of raw tobacco, soap and rattlesnake heads boiled up in a cauldron, fortified with wood alcohol and strained through the barman's undershirt. God only knew what it did to their insides: what it did to their tempers could be gauged by counting the tombstones in the town's Boot Hill.

Next, someone would open a general store, then a blacksmith would set up his forge, and after that the town would start to grow. How big depended on the local ranches. If they did well the town would boom. More saloons would open, maybe a hard-faced madam would bring her string of tired whores to town and open up a whorehouse.

When the cowhands tired of drink and women, they could lose money at the tables. In that kind of town only a fool expected to find an honest game, and only a brave man, and a gun-handy one, dared say he'd been cheated.

Soon the town would get a reputation for being rough, tough and never curried below the knees. Shootings and knifings would be daily events. The town's Boot Hill would fill up mighty fast.

That wouldn't last long. The shopkeepers would get together and appoint a tough sheriff with orders to clean up the town.

Once the gamblers and gunmen had been driven away the respectable citizens would build a school, maybe even a church. Then the town would be well on its way to becoming a city.

But from the look of it, Antelope Wells was going in the other direction.

Aaron Hunter huddled further into his heavy coat. He had a job to do and he'd better get on down there and do it. He dug his heels into his horse's flanks and trotted off down the trail.

The howling wind was behind him all the way down into Antelope Wells. The livery stable was shut up for the night. The water-trough outside was empty and dry. Fortunately for his horse, the saloon made a windbreak.

Hunter swung out of the saddle, twisted the reins round the hitching rail and left the poor animal to its own devices. He'd find somewhere to stable it later on. Right now he needed a drink. His throat was full of trail dust.

He pushed open the doors of the saloon and stepped inside. A silence fell. A dozen pairs of hard eyes regarded him appraisingly.

They saw a tall man, dressed in a long grey coat. His low-crowned black hat was tied under his chin with a black bandanna. His eyes were grey and cold.

Hunter unfastened the bandanna and shook it out, raising a miniature duststorm, before tucking it away in a pocket of his coat. He unfastened the coat, withdrew a coin from his vest pocket and tossed it on to the bar. 'Beer!' he demanded.

The burly, unshaven barkeep took one look at his expression and hurried to obey. He had seen men like this before. Sensible men didn't cross them unless they had a damn good reason, like a big bag of gold eagles. Even then they would do well to think twice.

Hunter took a long satisfying pull at his drink. His throat felt like he'd swallowed half the desert. The second pull drained the glass and he called for another, which went down his throat rather more slowly. Behind him, conversation started up again.

He crooked his finger at the barman. Curly Watts hurried along the bar. 'What'll it be,' he asked obsequiously, 'another beer, or a whiskey mebbe?'

'Neither,' Hunter replied in low tones, 'It's information I want.'

The barkeep seemed to shrink into himself. His eyes were frightened. 'I can't help you,' he stammered.

Hunter's eyebrows rose slightly. 'I haven't

asked you anything yet!'

'And when you do, I ain't answerin'!' was the scared reply.

Hunter was about to press him harder when he saw the man's eyes widen suddenly. He swung round. Two men had left their card game and had crossed the room towards him on silent feet. The barman's nervousness and his own quick reactions had stopped them dead in their tracks.

The men glowered at him, their hands hovering over their gunbutts. They were dressed like cowhands, but their gunbelts were a mite too fancy for real rannies and their boots were too shiny for men just in off the range.

Hunter sighted inwardly. He had hoped to make a quiet entrance to the valley. But it was not to be. He'd only been in town five minutes and he was already in trouble. He glanced round the room. None of the men at the tables would meet his eyes.

Hunter realized that they were all too scared of the gunmen to try and help him. And why should they, he thought wryly. They were townsmen. He was a stranger.

'Hey! You!' One of the gunmen, a smooth-faced young man whose twisted lip gave him an evil sneer, was the first to open the ball.

Hunter wasn't a bit impressed by this show of bravado. 'Are you talking to me, boy?' he said coldly.

The young man flushed. His hands, hovering over his gunbutts, twitched nervously. 'Yeah, old man, I was!' he sneered. 'We don't like strangers round here.'

'Especially strangers askin' questions,' his companion grated. 'If'n you know what's good for you you'll drink up and ride out of here pronto.'

Hunter smiled thinly. 'You boys are making a big mistake.'

'No mistake,' said the man with the twisted lip. 'Now git!'

'And what if I don't?'

'This!'

Both men went for their guns. But Hunter was faster. The two men had barely grasped their gunbutts before his gun cleared leather and swung up to cover them.

The two gunmen froze. The barrel of Hunter's Colt .44 looked as big as a mineshaft.

'Now let's have an end to this foolishness,' Hunter said levelly. 'Unbuckle your gunbelts and let them fall.' His cold eyes swept over the other men at the tables. 'The rest of you keep your hands where I can see them.'

As the two gunbelts fell to the floor with a clatter a low murmur of approval ran round the room. The two would-be gunmen had no friends in here, that was for sure.

Hunter smiled sardonically. 'Perhaps *now* someone will answer my questions?'

The barkeep seemed pleased at the two gunmen's discomfiture. 'You never got round to sayin' what they was,' he said with a broad grin. 'Nor who you are, neither.'

'No more I did,' Hunter agreed. 'The name is Hunter, Aaron Hunter; and I'm looking for Bill Lonegan.'

The older of the two gunmen guffawed loudly. 'Then you're plumb out of luck, stranger.'

'How so?' demanded Hunter, though the gunman's gloating tone had already given him the answer.

'He was shot dead a fortnight ago.'

Hunter's eyes narrowed angrily and the hardcase felt a shiver of fear run up his spine. He cocked a questioning eye at the barkeep who nodded his confirmation of the man's story. He turned back to face the gloating gunman.

'You shot him?'

'Hell no,' the man replied with false bravado. 'Ben Strutt did it.' His mouth

13

twisted in a sneer. 'If you brace him with it he'll kill you too, and I hope to God I'm there to see it.'

Hunter's mouth tightened angrily. 'You won't be. You're leaving this valley today. If I see you again I'll kill you. And your friend. Now pick up your guns and get out of here.'

The two men glanced briefly at one another, cautiously picked up their guns and backed out of the saloon.

Hunter holstered his gun and leaned back against the bar. Some of the other men got up from the tables and clustered round him admiringly. Hunter hid his contempt for these fair-weather friends behind a bland smile.

'So Bill Lonegan is dead is he?' he said casually. 'How'd it happen, barkeep?'

'Strutt picked a fight with Bill and shot him down like a dog. Bill didn't have a chance. He was a good man, but he sure weren't no gunfighter. Strutt put two bullets in his brisket before Bill even cleared leather.'

'Is this Strutt a townsman, or a local rancher?'

'Naw. He rides for Bricklin,' one of the other men informed him. There was a touch of envy in his voice as he went on: 'Bricklin's

14

the biggest rancher hereabouts. Got him a spread way down the valley. He's got the best land, best water and the best cattle too.'

'Don't ferget his hands,' a gnarled oldster added dryly. 'He's got plenty of 'em and they're all right gunhandy. Mind you, Ben Strutt's the best of 'em by a mile!'

'Those two you braced just now work for Bricklin,' a third man declared slyly. 'Deke Bricklin sends his boys into town now and again to throw their weight around and remind us just who's the boss around here.'

'He'll be fit to be tied when he hears how you made them two take water,' chuckled the whiskery oldster. 'He pays fer the best and aims to git it too. Them boys all knows that if they cain't make good on their boasts they can draw their time and git.'

'So Bricklin's the bull of the woods round here?'

'You'd better believe it, brother.'

'I guess he doesn't spend much money in town,' said Hunter, glancing round at the shabby furnishings of the saloon and the worn out clothes of the men clustered round him at the bar.

That wiped the grins off their faces. 'Yer right. He don't,' volunteered the barman. 'The old devil does all his buyin' over the hills in Mariposa.'

'Why's that?' Hunter asked curiously.

'Gittin' his revenge on the town, most likely,' one of the men said sourly. 'The bastard thought he'd like fine to be mayor of Antelope Wells, reckoned it'd make him look good when he went up to the county seat on business, I guess. Waal, he didn't reckon on your friend Lonegan, did he?'

Hunter's eyebrows rose. Now they were getting to it. 'What had Lonegan got to do with it?'

'Only stood up against Bricklin, and won,' the bartender said admiringly. 'Us towns-people don't cotton much to Bricklin and his bullyboys.'

There was a growl of agreement from the other men.

'So we all voted for Lonegan.'

The barkeep smiled broadly as he remembered the rancher's incredulous face when the votes were counted. The valley's richest man had been so sure he would win that he hadn't even bothered to get his men to bribe or threaten the voters.

'Bricklin was fit to be tied. He swore he'd get even with Lonegan. Meanwhile, he was damn well gonna take his business to a town that'd appreciate it.'

16

He grimaced sourly. 'That's when Antelope Wells began to die. Without Bricklin's business the town couldn't support two stores...'

'Hell, Curly!' a man dressed as a storekeeper interjected glumly. 'It cain't even support one. And I ought to know!'

'I guess that's true enough, Mr Chapman,' Curly replied with a grin. 'Anyways, within a week Robsart ups stakes and moves his store to Mariposa. One of the two livery stables closed soon after that. Since then it's been downhill all the way. There's still a little business done around here, the smaller ranchers ain't under Bricklin's thumb just yet, but there's not nearly enuff to keep us goin'.'

'I guess it won't be long before we go under fer good,' storekeeper Chapman said resentfully. 'If I had anywhere else to go I'd have gone already!'

'Then there's no demand for a preacher hereabouts?' Hunter said dryly.

The townsmen guffawed loudly. 'A preacher? You must be plumb crazy,' said one satirically. 'What the hell would a preacher find to do round here? Preach forgiveness to old man Bricklin?'

'There's a fair bit of buryin', one way and

another,' laughed his friend Harry Rose, known as Rosey. 'And there'll soon be more if those damn nesters don't up stakes and move on right quick.'

'Nesters?' Hunter raised his eyebrows.

'Yeah,' a third man pushed to the front, eager to add his two cents worth of gossip to the heap. 'A bunch of sodbusters moved into the valley a week ago. Squatted down in the valley bottom by the river. Started puttin' up soddy huts.'

Rosey elbowed him aside. 'Iffen they ain't shifted quick, they'll be puttin' their ploughs into our good range,' he interrupted sourly. 'Before we know it they'll be stringing wire everywheres. God knows there ain't much ter be said fer Bricklin, but he sure knows what to do with sodbusters. He's given 'em a week to get out. If they ain't moved by then he swears he'll burn 'em out.'

'I'd have thought you'd welcome the farmers,' Hunter remarked quietly. 'You've lost Bricklin's business. Maybe they can take his place. They'll want supplies, won't they?'

That thought didn't seem to have occurred to any of the men before. Their mouths fell open.

Curly scratched his bald head thoughtfully. 'Well, that's a thought, surely it is,' he said. 'Maybe it's the farmers that'll be the saving of this town. Sure as hell the ranchers ain't doin' it any good.'

'If they'd spend money in my store I'll get down on my knees and kiss their muddy boots so help me,' said Chapman the store-keeper, drawing a roar of laughter from his fellow townsmen.

Hunter saw that he had swung the saloon loafers round to his way of thinking. 'Then if the town is not going to die after all,' he said blandly, 'maybe it'll need a preacher?'

'Why the hell do you keep goin' on about preachers?' demanded Rosey. 'Do you happen to know a bible-puncher who's lookin' for a job right now?'

'Yes, me!' Hunter replied with a sardonic grin.

That rocked his hearers back on their heels.

'You?'

'I just said so, didn't I?'

'But preachers don't use a gun like you do!'

'Some do, and I'm one of them.'

'Then I guess Antelope Wells has got itself a preacher, eh boys?' Rosey declared loudly, and his friends agreed in a roar of good

19

feeling. None of them had heard the stranger preach, but that didn't matter a bit; he was good with a gun, and it seemed he was willing to help them stand up to Bricklin. That was enough to make them want him to stay in Antelope Wells.

'Right then,' Hunter said when the noise finally died down. 'Tell me about Lonegan.'

'Was he a friend of yours?' said the barman curiously.

'Not especially,' Hunter replied evenly. 'He was going to give me a job.'

'As preacher?' the storekeeper remarked with a derisive smile.

'No. As town marshal!'

The men exchanged startled glances. The job was vacant, sure enough. The last man to wear the badge had resigned rather than take on Bricklin and his men. They knew nothing about this man. But they sure as hell needed a marshal. Maybe the stranger could manage to stay alive long enough to bring law and order to Antelope Wells.

'Man,' the bartender breathed respect-fully, 'you sure do like livin' dangerously. You start wearin' a badge in this town and Bricklin'll have your hide nailed to his barn door inside a week!'

'He can try,' Hunter said calmly.

'Have you got any experience of mar-shalin'?'

'A little,' Hunter replied coolly. He reached into a pocket and pulled out a badge. They all recognized the silver star in a circle badge issued to US deputy marshals.

'Fair enough,' Curly acknowledged. 'They don't hand those out to just anyone.'

'No, they don't,' Hunter agreed. 'Now let's get things straight. I came here to do a job. Lonegan is dead, so I guess you've got no mayor to make it official.'

'That's right,' Mr Chapman declared with a puzzled frown. 'So what?'

'Then why not give me the job?'

That caused a buzz of comment, heads were scratched and voices raised in animated discussion while Hunter sipped his beer, a sardonic smile on his face.

'We're all in favour,' said Chapman, who had been tacitly elected spokesman for the group. 'But there's one problem. According to the town rules, the mayor has to be a property owner.'

'I guess there are plenty of empty prop-erties in town right now,' Hunter responded dryly, 'and I'll be needing a place to hold Sunday meeting. Why don't you sell me one of the empty shacks?'

That struck everyone as a damned good idea, and a deal was swiftly struck. For ten dollars and other valuable considerations, as the legal phrase has it, Hunter became the proud owner of a dilapidated barn on the outskirts of town.

'Make a fine church, with a bit of work,' the former owner guffawed. He had never thought he would get a buyer. He'd been letting the building fall down by itself.

'Right,' said Hunter. 'Now I'm a property owner. Next business!'

The town's doctor, a man respected by everyone, banged his empty beer glass on the bar counter until a silence fell. 'I declare this election open,' he said. 'Are there any nominations for the vacant post of mayor of Antelope Wells?'

'I nominate Mr Hunter,' John Chapman said primly.

'Seconded,' piped up Jim Bacher the town's whiskery old carpenter, wheelwright, and general handyman.

'Any further nominations?' asked the doctor. The room was silent. 'Then I declare Mr Aaron Hunter duly elected mayor of Antelope Wells.'

The announcement was greeted with cheers.

'Next business!' bawled Rio Harkness. 'We want Mr Hunter here to be our town marshal too, don't we?' There was a general cry of agreement. 'Then I say he's elected. All in favour raise your hands!'

The election was ratified without a dissenting voice.

Hunter bowed slightly. 'I thank you for your confidence in me,' he said evenly. He knew damned well that they had turned to him in sheer desperation. They'd probably expect him to fight Bricklin and his men on his own. If they'd been fighters they would have done something to defend their town against the rancher already.

Then he decided to give them the benefit of the doubt. Maybe all they needed was a leader. Many men would fight bravely if well led who would act the coward if forced to fight alone. It was his job to give this town and its people the leadership they needed.

Now that the fateful decisions had been taken the townsmen pressed Hunter to drink with them but he refused. 'I need to stable my horse,' he declared. 'It's been outside, eating dust, all this time.'

'I done lost the key to your new property, Mr Mayor,' laughed the vendor, 'but I guess you can break the lock if you wants to.'

Hunter nodded. 'I guess I can at that.' He took a couple of steps towards the door, then turned back. 'Where can I get a bite to eat round here?'

'Mrs Considine runs a pretty good diner,' the doctor informed him. 'But she'll be closed up now.'

'I can do you a steak,' Curly offered, always eager to please.

'Good. In about half an hour?'

'Sure thing.'

'Right, see you later,' said Hunter, and left the saloon.

The two gunmen were waiting outside in the dark street. The young man with the twisted lip opened the ball. He drew his six-gun and triggered a shot at Hunter as he came through the lighted doorway. His partner fired a split second later.

But Hunter had been half expecting them to try and bushwhack him. As the two tongues of flame split the night he dived to the ground and rolled into the shadows. The gunmen's bullets screamed over his head and on into the saloon, making the drinkers hurriedly dive for cover under the tables.

The two men fired again. Hot lead missed Hunter by a whisker and slammed into the wall of the saloon, piercing two neat holes in the weatherbeaten planks.

That was too close for comfort! Hunter palmed his .44 and fired at the nearest muzzle flash. The gunman caught the lump of spinning lead in the belly. He gave a high-pitched cry of agony and folded over the wound, dropping his gun, then fell to his knees in the dusty street.

Hunter's next shot hit the man with the twisted lip in the head. The back of the gunman's skull blew out in a shower of blood and brains. He fell to the ground without a sound.

As the echoes died away the townsmen cowering inside the saloon looked at each other apprehensively. Was their new mayor and marshal dead already?

The saloon doors swung open and Hunter pushed his way into the room, bringing with him the sharp smell of gunsmoke.

Some of the men felt a chill run up their spines. In his black clothes Hunter looked like the angel of death himself. Now he had brought real death to their little town.

'Is there an undertaker in town?' Hunter asked levelly.

'No there ain't,' admitted Curly Watts, still half in shock. 'Not now, anyways. He moved to Mariposa with the other cowards. But I guess Jim Bacher here could knock you up a box.'

He indicated the whiskery old-timer nursing a drink at one of the tables. 'He's our carpenter. He put up most of the buildings round here.'

Hunter looked inquiringly at the oldster.

'Sure mister. I can make you a coffin,' he cackled.

'Better make it two,' Hunter replied dryly. 'Bricklin's men?'

'That's right. I guess they hoped to get even,' Hunter replied grimly. 'Instead they got dead.' He turned towards the door. 'Don't forget, now. Half an hour for that steak.'

'Yes Sir!' Curly ejaculated respectfully. 'Yes Sir!'

TWO

Hunter spent the night in his new property, bedded in the stale straw with his horse. The animal was a good sentry. With it on guard he could get a good night's sleep.

Next morning bright and early he washed under the pump, shaved his bristly chin and brushed the worst of the trail dust from his clothes. Last night he had met the men of the town. This morning their womenfolk would be giving him the once over.

As Hunter walked down to saloon for breakfast women watched him from doorways and peered at him through the shop windows. A couple of the braver ones tripped innocently out of Chapman's General Store and came towards him, chattering brightly to each other.

Hunter smiled and tipped his hat. The two young women bobbed their heads, flushed and hurried on down the street. Hunter knew they hadn't gone far before turning to stare after him. He could feel their eyes on his back. They would start talking about him as soon as he had disappeared into the saloon.

The barman had a broad smile on his face. 'Breakfast, Marshal?' he said cheerfully. 'There's steak, tortillas and beans. The coffee's fit to float an anvil. Made it fresh this morning. And you could have a pancake to follow if you wanted.'

'That'll be fine,' Hunter said agreeably, and taking a seat at one of the tables, began to roll himself a smoke.

After breakfast Hunter thought he'd examine the jailhouse. He might be needing it soon. He asked Curly where it was.

'There ain't no jail in Antelope Wells.' Curly gave the bartop a desultory wipe with a rag that looked as if it was last washed to celebrate Lincoln's inauguration. 'Not no more, anyways. When the last marshal done run out on us some of Bricklin's men set it afire by way o' celebratin' the event.'

Hunter rubbed his chin thoughtfully. What kind of town was this? No mayor, no marshal, and now no jail! 'Don't tell me there's no blacksmith either?' he said derisively.

'Of course there is,' Curly was quick to defend the honour of Antelope Wells. 'You'll find him down the other end of town. His name's Somers, Obadiah Somers. He's a damn fine blacksmith and a pretty good man all round!'

Hunter rose to his feet and glanced round the saloon. A few loafers had come in while he was having breakfast. 'Anyone want to earn a dollar?' he asked.

'Doin' what?' Rio Harkness replied cautiously.

'I want someone to go out to the Bricklin ranch and tell Bricklin what happened last night.'

'Man, I'd do that fer nothin,' the young cowboy replied with a grin. 'It'll be worth the ride seein' Bricklin's face when he gets the news. He'll be fit to be tied.'

Hunter's lips twisted cynically. 'If I were you I'd not let him see you smiling. Just tell him the funeral's set for midday. He's welcome to attend if he wants to.'

He felt in his vest pocket for a dollar and flipped it across the room. The young cowboy caught it on the fly, bit it and slipped it into his jeans pocket.

The two men left the saloon together. Harkness unhitched his horse from the rail and tipping his hat to Hunter, clattered off down the street. Hunter followed more slowly, on foot.

As he walked down the street Hunter examined all the buildings carefully. Many of them were empty. Curly Watts had told him that the weaklings amongst the shopkeepers had already left Antelope Wells, scared off by Bricklin's threats. It seemed he was right.

From the look of things the remaining businesses were barely making ends meet. Outside the general store a wagon was being loaded with supplies. Another stood waiting for the doctor to come out of the gunsmith's, whose wife was expecting a baby. A few horses were standing at the hitching rails along the street, and that was all.

A town like this, set in the middle of a fertile valley with six or seven ranches round about it, ought to be buzzing with life. Instead it was more than half dead. If the smaller ranchers stopped sending their men into town to do their buying the remaining businesses would close. The people would move away and Antelope Wells would become a ghost town.

Last week two cowboys from the Lazy J ranch had come into town for a drink. They had been prodded into a fight and shot down by a couple of Bricklin's gunmen. The town hadn't seen a rider from one of the smaller ranches since then.

Hunter knew he would have to ride out to see the ranchers and try to persuade them it was safe to send their men back to town. But would they listen? Probably not.

Bill Lonegan had tried to stand up to Bricklin and his reward had been two bullets in the belly and a grave in Boot Hill. Now it was up to him, Aaron Hunter, to do what had to be done. Bricklin had the town by the throat. Men would have to die before he would loosen his grip.

The blacksmith was a short man, but made up for it in girth. His chest was like a beer-barrel and his belly thrust against his leather apron. His bare arms were corded with muscle. He held the ten-pound sledge as lightly as if it were a flywhisk.

As Hunter entered the smithy he brought the hammer down on to the anvil with a crash that made the marshal's ears ring. Sparks flew high in the air. The blacksmith laid the hammer aside, peered at the twisted piece of metal he had just hit, nodded approvingly, grasped it in a pair of tongs and dropped it into a barrel of water standing nearby. There was a violent hiss and a cloud of steam.

'Well, Marshal?' he growled. 'What can I

do for you?'

'Make me a set of fetters!'

The blacksmith scratched his head. 'I can do that, right enough. But why the hell do you want fetters?'

'I might need to keep someone safe,' said Hunter, 'and there's no jail in Antelope Wells.'

The blacksmith put his hands on his hips and laughed heartily. 'Not since Bricklin's men run our last marshal out of town, there ain't! You expectin' to do better?'

Hunter shrugged. 'I aim to try.'

'Then I'll make 'em for ye. When do ye want 'em?'

'Today?'

'I'll do me best.'

'Fair enough.' Hunter put out his hand and the other man took it.

'Good luck, Marshal,' the blacksmith said seriously. 'You'll need it.'

'I've got God on my side,' replied Hunter evenly. 'I don't need luck.' He turned on his heel and left the smithy.

The blacksmith watched him go with a worried look on his face. Faith was all very well for Easterners and soft city dwellers, but out here in the West if men weren't lucky they usually didn't get to live very long. By refusing to ask Lady Luck for help Hunter was asking for trouble.

The blacksmith wondered if it was worth making the fetters, then remembered the look in Hunter's eye and decided to do as he was asked. Men like Hunter made their own luck.

The building next to the blacksmith's was a livery stable. Hunter went inside and greeted the owner, whom he remembered as one of the faces in the saloon last night. The name on the board over the door was Mark Tiverton. He was a complete contrast to the blacksmith, being as tall and thin as a lodge-pole pine.

His eyes lit up when he saw Hunter. 'Want me to look after your horse, Marshal? Two bits a day and all the oats he can eat.'

It was a pretty good deal and Hunter closed with it on the spot.

'Where do you get your oats?' Hunter asked casually.

'They're shipped in from Denver,' the man replied with surprise. 'Why d'you ask?'

'I was wondering if the farmers were planning on planting oats,' Hunters said. 'If they are, would you buy?'

The man sucked in his cheeks. 'Mebbe I would at that. If the price was right.'

'Good. I'll tell them.'

Antelope Well's new marshal continued on down the street. The next three buildings were empty and derelict. Beyond them the level plain stretched away into the misty distance. It was all Bricklin land in this direction. Any attack on the town would probably come this way.

The shacks on the other side of the street were occupied by poor families, whose breadwinners normally worked as ostlers, store clerks, labourers and similar. Most of these men were out of work. Their shacks were all they owned. If they left town they would have nothing. So they stayed, hoping for better times, while their scrawny wives and round-eyed children grew thinner and thinner.

Hunter walked back up the street, following the sound of hammering. He pushed open the door of a shed and went inside. Jim Bacher was knocking nails into a rough wooden box resting on a pair of trestles in the middle of the floor. A second box leaned against the wall.

The bodies of the two gunmen Hunter had shot the previous night lay together by the wall. Their faces were waxy and their cheeks had already begun to fall in.

Bacher looked up as Hunter entered his workshop. ''Mornin', Marshal,' he said cheerfully. 'Soon be finished with this here box. You'll want to bury 'em quick, I'm thinkin'. It's gonna be hot later on today.'

Hunter's mouth twisted sourly. He never killed a man without regretting the necessity that had driven him to it and the wasted life he had just ended so violently. These two men had chosen the wrong path and had paid for it. All debts were now settled, in this world, if not the next. They had the right to be buried with dignity.

Hunter stripped the gunbelts from the bodies and searched their pockets carefully. The younger of the two men had three gold eagles in one pocket, and a thin packet of letters in the other. With luck Hunter would be able to send word of this man's death to his next of kin.

Most lawmen didn't bother with such niceties. They burnt any letters they found and appropriated anything that was worth having.

The other man had five gold eagles in his vest pocket but no letters or other means of identification.

The gold was a message in itself. Most cowhands made thirty dollars a month at best, and got their pay in smaller notes and coins that were much easier to spend. Bricklin had urged these men on to their deaths with gold.

'Have you got a couple of burlap bags I can borrow?' Hunter asked the carpenter, piling the men's possessions in two neat heaps.

'Ain't ye goin' ter take their boots?' the old man cackled. 'From the look of 'em they're almost new!'

'They died in them, they'll be buried in them,' Hunter replied coldly. 'Haven't you got any respect for the dead?'

The old man's weatherbeaten face darkened angrily. 'It's all right fer you, Mister Marshal,' he growled, as he tossed Hunter two small sacks and turned back to his carpentry. 'You ain't been bullied an' chivied and had yer town run down almost ter nuffin' by these two young gunnies and their friends or you'd be minded to dance on their graves like the rest of us!' He sighed heavily. 'But I guess you're right at that.'

Hunter put the men's effects into the two bags. 'Talking of graves, I take it you've sent someone up to Boot Hill to dig graves for these two men.'

'Sure thing. Young Billy has been up there

since sunup. He's a bit slow in his thinkin' is Billy, but he's a damn good man with a shovel.'

He knocked in the last nail and straightened up, favouring his aching back. 'There, that's done.' He grinned slyly at Hunter. 'You gonna help me put 'em in their boxes?'

'Of course.'

Hunter grasped the first body under the arms and Bacher took its feet. They lifted the corpse and laid it down in the coffin. Then they did the same with the other body. Then Bacher took up his hammer and nailed the lids down.

'Just you wait there a mite and I'll bring the buckboard round to the front of the building,' said Bacher, and off he went.

When the two men had loaded the coffins on to the buckboard, Bacher climbed on to the seat and took the reins. Hunter took off his gunbelt, rolled it up, and put it under the seat. Then he got up beside the old carpenter.

'Straight up to Boot Hill?' queried Bacher.

'Stop outside the saloon first.'

Bacher raised his bushy eyebrows, but said nothing. He shook the reins and the horse ambled up the dusty street.

At this time of day anyone who had work

to do was doing it. The men in the saloon were all loafers from the cabins at the end of town. They were nursing their drinks to make them last as long as possible.

Hunter nodded to Curly Watts and then turned to face the room. 'I'm going up to Boot Hill to bury those two gunnies I shot yesterday,' he said evenly, 'I want six men to act as pall-bearers.'

'For Bricklin's men?' a voice called out derisively. 'Hell no!'

'For those human beings,' Hunter replied harshly. 'You'll do for one of the pall-bearers. On your feet!'

The loafer saw the look in Hunter's eye and hurriedly got up. Hunter eyed the man's companions. 'And the rest of you! You ain't much, but Gideon made do with worse.'

Hunter strode towards the door, followed by the six men he had chosen. Those who remained looked at each other speculatively.

'Do you think Deke Bricklin'll come to the buryin'?' one of them said thoughtfully.

'The marshal sent Rio out there to tell him special,' another man replied. The two men exchanged amused glances, then got up and headed for the door.

'I ain't missin' this,' declared Curly Watts

to the room at large. 'Drink up and get out of here, you fellas. The bar's closed 'til further notice!'

The buckboard rolled up the street with Jim Bacher at the reins. Aaron Hunter sat beside him. On the flatbed behind them were the two rough wooden coffins. The six pall-bearers shuffled along beside the buckboard. Curly Watts and the drinkers from the saloon walked behind them.

As they passed the general store John Chapman was serving old Mrs Rossiter, who gave the town's children such schooling as their parents were prepared to pay for, which wasn't much. Her clothes were shiny with age, though they were always painfully clean and carefully darned. Her perfect manners and cultivated accents showed that she had once seen better days.

The storekeeper saw the procession go past and his eyebrows nearly met his hairline. He called his young assistant out of the storeroom, hastily instructed him to take Mrs Rossiter's order, whipped off his apron, donned his suitcoat, and ran out of the door after the cortège.

The doctor had been making another visit to the gunsmith's wife, whose baby was slow in arriving. Dardick was just showing him out of his shop as the procession rolled past. The two men exchanged incredulous glances, then stepped down into the street and joined the crowd following on behind the buckboard.

The same story was repeated over and over again as the cortège rolled along the street. By the time the procession passed the last tumbledown shacks on the edge of town and headed for God's Acre, almost all the able-bodied men in town were following on behind, either on foot or on horseback. They were accompanied by all those children who had managed to escape their mothers' clutches. With the exception of the blacksmith, busy making a set of iron fetters, Antelope Wells was left to its women.

The town's Boot Hill was situated on a piece of rising ground a couple of hundred yards from edge of town. There was no fence. It was merely a patch of hummocky ground with twenty or thirty wooden markers, some standing upright, some leaning drunkenly. There were two freshly dug graves, each with its adjacent heap of sandy soil. Young Billy, the town's half-wit, stood beside them proudly, leaning on his shovel.

'I done 'em, Mister Bacher,' he said in his

40

squeaky tenor. 'Good and deep, like you said. Those gunnies won't get out. Not till Judgement Day they won't.'

'There's a good lad,' said Jim Bacher approvingly. 'Now come and hold the horse's head until we've done buryin' 'em.'

Billy dropped the shovel by the grave and did as he was told. Bacher let go of the reins and got down from the buckboard. He went to the flat-bed and took out three stout ropes which he laid on the ground beside the first grave.

Hunter climbed down from the buckboard and gestured to his six unwilling pall-bearers. They pulled one of the coffins off the flat-bed and hoisted it on to their shoulders, then carried it to the grave and laid it down on the ropes.

At a further command from Hunter they took hold of the ends of the ropes and slowly lowered it into the grave. Then they repeated the process with the second coffin.

The townspeople clustered round the foot of the two open graves. Hunter removed his hat and laid it aside. Taking the hint, the men removed their hats and held them in their hands. Hunter took a prayer book from his pocket and began to intone the burial service in his strong deep voice.

Most of his audience had come to this funeral out of curiosity, not religious feeling, but Hunter managed to infuse his reading with such emotional power that even the most cynical of his hearers was gripped by the beauty of Cranmer's words.

The men who were being buried were hired killers, yes; but they were also someone's child, someone's brother, someone's father, even.

The members of Hunter's audience knew that death could come to each of them as easily and unexpectedly as it had come to these two gunmen. When Hunter intoned the last amen he was joined by most of the men clustered round the graves.

The solemn mood was suddenly broken as Herb Bricklin and ten of his father's men rode up in a cloud of dust. The young rancher snapped his fingers and his men spread out on either side of him.

The assembled townspeople glanced nervously from Hunter to young Bricklin and back again. Hunter seemed unmoved and they took strength from him.

Bricklin was a burly man in his early twenties with a face like a fist and a manner to match. His men were mostly hardcases with tied-down guns and bitter expressions.

'Those my pa's men you were buryin',
preacher?' he grated.

'If you're a Bricklin, then yes, they were,'
Hunter replied evenly.

'Who killed them?'

'I did.'

The rancher's gunmen eyed Hunter with
new interest. Had the stranger in preacher's
duds really killed Kit Berry and Bunco
Green. They had been pretty quick on the
draw. This man wasn't even wearing a gun.
Preachers never did. They didn't go around
shooting gunmen either. If anything, it was
the other way about.

Herb Bricklin goggled at Hunter. 'You
killed Berry and Green?' he cried incredulously. 'I don't believe it. You're
sheltering someone. Tell me who it is or I'll
shoot you down where you stand, preacher
or no preacher.'

Hunter shook his head. 'No you won't,' he
said calmly. 'But I'll tell you what you will
do. You'll go back to your pa and tell him to
pay off his gunmen, stop bullying this town,
and start trying to be a good neighbour to
everyone in this valley.'

Herb Bricklin's face went purple with rage.
'I'm damned if I will,' he yelled hoarsely.

'You'll be damned if you don't,' Hunter

replied levelly. 'Your pa's lost two men already. How many more will he have to lose before he sees sense?'

'Sees sense?' snarled Bricklin. He slewed round in his saddle to face the crowd of townspeople. 'Listen up, you people. Pa offered to be your friend, but you chose Lonegan instead. Well, he's dead now, so that's that. Pa's willing to give you lot another chance. But you'll have to get rid of this bigmouth first.' His angry eyes swept across the band of townspeople. 'Well, what do you say?'

His men grinned maliciously at the assembled townspeople and fingered their guns. The message was clear. Go with Bricklin or face a gun battle, either here and now or later on. The crowd swayed uncertainly, like grass blown by the wind.

Hunter wondered what they would decide to do. Had his arrival in town given these mice enough backbone to nerve them to try and bell the cat?

Doctor Thompson broke the silence. 'Last night we elected a new mayor,' he said with a chuckle. '*And* a new marshal.'

'We got pretty good value for money, too,' John Chapman spoke up boldly. He'd lost more than anyone by Deke Bricklin's actions and was more than willing to rub the rancher's nose in the dirt now the chance had come. 'They're the same man, *and* we got the preacher here as boot on the deal. Your pa can't offer us anything half as good, now can he, Herb?'

There was a moment of silence as Chapman's words sank in, then the assembled townspeople began to laugh.

Herb Bricklin wasn't the kind of man to enjoy being made a fool of. He glared at the defiant storekeeper and the smiling doctor. But he knew damn well who had revived the townsmen's fighting spirit.

'You're behind all this,' he grated, swinging round to face the black-clad preacher. 'These tenderfeet haven't the sand to buck Pa by their own selves.' An evil smile spread across his unlovely features. 'When you're dead they'll soon back down again.'

Without any more warning his hand flashed for his gun.

As Bricklin made his move Aaron Hunter drew a short-barrelled Webley Bulldog pistol from under his coat. He wasn't the man to wear a gunbelt to a funeral, but he had too much savvy to go anywhere unarmed.

Herb Bricklin's own pistol had only just

cleared leather when the preacher's Bulldog barked and he felt a smashing blow on the hand. He screamed with pain and his pearlhandled Colt went flying.

The gunmen had been caught by surprise by their leader's action. Deke Bricklin had told his son to attend the funeral in order to find out who had killed his two men. He didn't believe the young cowboy's tale of a gun-handy preacher come out of nowhere to save Antelope Wells. He thought the townsmen must have hired a gunfighter, and wanted to know who he was up against before sending any more of his own men to brace him. If the man was a known killer it might be better to have him shot in the back. Herb wasn't supposed to start any gunplay, and the men with him knew it.

Right now the preacher was the master of the situation. His pistol was out and pointed straight between Herb's eyes. His gunmen's weapons were still in their holsters. Long before any of them could draw and fire their boss's son would be down and dead. They scowled at Hunter but kept their hands well clear of their guns.

Tears of rage and pain were running down Herb Bricklin's fleshy cheeks. 'My pa'll kill you for this,' he grated.

'No doubt he'll try,' Hunter replied evenly. 'But right now I've got the edge.'

'Maybe so,' sneered Bricklin, 'but you lose that the moment I ride out of here.'

'That's why you're coming back to town with me.'

'Why the hell should I?' Herb demanded.

Hunter smiled thinly. 'Because I'm the man holding the gun.'

The townspeople laughed heartily at this sally. Hunter sure was livening things up around Antelope Wells.

Then the laughter died as they realized the implications of his remark. Why the hell did he want to bring young Bricklin into town? Surely it was only asking for trouble? They began to mutter amongst themselves. Hunter was going too far, and much too fast, for their liking.

The group of gunmen had been wondering what the black-clad preacher meant to do with their boss's son. Now one of them spoke up strongly. He wore a black-and-white cowhide vest and striped pants. Hunter didn't know him, but the townsmen sure did. This was Ben Strutt, Bricklin's head honcho.

'You know we'll come after him, don't you, Preacher!' he said, and his angry eyes raked the assembled townsmen. 'Deke Bricklin has got more'n thirty men on his payroll, and they're all damn good with their guns. If we come to town a lot of you men are going to die. I say you'd better let Herb go!'

The townsmen shuffled their feet nervously. They didn't like the sound of that at all. Ben Strutt was a cold-hearted killer and the men behind him were almost as bad!

'And I say he's our hostage for your boss's good behaviour,' Hunter countered. 'Go back to the ranch and tell him so. If he tries to attack Antelope Wells his son will be the first to catch a bullet. And that's a promise.'

'I hear you,' the gunman said sourly. He wheeled his horse round to face the way he'd come. 'OK boys. Back to the ranch!'

The gunman took off in a cloud of dust, followed by angry cries from their boss's son. The townsmen heaved sighs of relief to see them go.

'You sure like living on the edge, don't you, Marshal?' chuckled Doc Thompson.

'As we read in Psalm 27 verse 1, "The Lord is my strength, of whom shall I be afraid"?' Hunter replied with a twinkle in his eyes. He gestured with the barrel of his pistol at Herb Bricklin. 'Turn that horse and walk in front of me.'

Scowling, the young rancher did as he was told. The remainder of the crowd followed him and Hunter back to town, leaving young Billy to fill in the two graves.

The townspeople talked amongst themselves in low voices as they walked back to town. They weren't at all sure that Hunter was doing the right thing, but at least he was doing something. Deke Bricklin had been pushing them around for months. Now at last they were pushing back.

When they got back to town Hunter sent a boy running down to the blacksmith's forge to ask whether the fetters were ready yet.

The blacksmith brought them himself, and despite Herb Bricklin's blood-curdling threats, cold-riveted the shackles round the young man's ankles and padlocked the other end of the chain to the stout wooden water-trough outside the saloon.

Scowling, Herb squatted down on the dusty ground and leaned his back against the water-trough.

'If your father's men hadn't burned down the jail,' Hunter said with a smile, 'you would be much more comfortable. As the Good Book says, "The sins of the fathers shall be visited on the children".'

He went into the saloon with the young man's vivid curses ringing in his ears.

THREE

The men who had accompanied Hunter to Boot Hill poured into the saloon and demanded drinks. Curly was almost rushed off his feet serving them, but he didn't mind a bit. Hunter was good for business.

While the townsmen celebrated Herb Bricklin's defeat and praised Hunter to the skies the man himself was making his way down the street to Mrs Considine's diner.

Mrs Considine was a cheerful Irishwoman with a body like a bolster, a face like a dumpling and hands like hams. Her daughter was a willowy creature with her mother's red hair and a scatter of freckles across her nose. Both women were as handy with a rolling-pin as a skillet. There was never any trouble in their establishment.

'Top o' the mornin', Marshal,' said Mrs Considine in a broad Irish accent. 'I was wonderin' how long ye'd be able to stand eatin' the muck Curly Watts dishes up. Sit ye down an' me daughter Mary'll bring ye a plate of proper grub!'

51

Mary Considine gave the handsome marshal a rogueish glance from under her long lashes and sashayed away into the kitchen.

'I see you got Herb Bricklin chained up out there like a dawg,' Mrs Considine said with a grin. 'That'll keep the old man off our backs, right enough. But fer how long, eh, Marshal?'

'That's a good question, Mrs Considine,' Hunter replied levelly. 'I'm hoping it'll keep Deke Bricklin quiet until I can make him see sense.'

'And how are ye goin' to do that?' the old woman said sceptically. 'Bricklin has always been top dawg round here. He won't give that up without a fight. He's a hard man, Marshal, with no give in him. He'll break before he bends, an' he'll take a deal o' breakin'.'

Hunter sighed heavily. 'I know the type. But he must either bend or break, if this country is to grow. There's no room in the West for men of his stripe any more.'

'Agreed!' Doctor Thompson had entered the diner just in time to hear Hunter's remark. 'Men like Bricklin aim to set themselves up as great lords with their own private armies the way it was in the old country,' he went on. 'Well, we're having none of that. This is a land where the little man can make it if he's willing to work hard.'

'Like the nesters?' Hunter said evenly.

Doctor Thompson chuckled richly. 'Yes. Like the nesters. The future of this country belongs to men who are willing to get down in the dirt and grow things. Ranchers like Bricklin are living in the past.'

Mary Considine swept out of the kitchen with a plate in one hand and a bundle of knives and forks in the other.

'I'd never marry a grubby farmer with dirt under his nails,' she said scathingly. 'If that's the way things are goin' I'm movin' to the city as soon as ever I can. So there!' She slapped Hunter's plate down in front of him with a crash and stalked off into the kitchen.

Doctor Thompson winked at Hunter, 'That girl is husband-high and just itching to be wed,' her chortled. 'I'd watch out if I were you, marshal.'

Hunter smiled enigmatically. He was too old to be caught so easily by a pretty face, even if she could cook like an angel. And her mother was a dreadful warning of what forty years of such cooking could do to a woman's figure.

Thompson sat down opposite Hunter.

'Despite what I said just now,' he began seriously, 'the ranchers are the key to this situation.'

'How so?'

'The smaller ranchers don't like Bricklin any more than the townspeople do. They can't face him alone, any of them, but if they'd only work together they could make him back off.'

He threw himself back in his chair and scratched his head, 'I'm asking you to go out and see them, marshal. Get them to join us against Bricklin. And make it soon. The town needs their business.'

Hunter regarded him thoughtfully for a moment. 'What do they think of the nesters?'

'Hate them, of course. Ranchers always hate nesters. If Bricklin hadn't been pressing them so hard they would have tried to run the nesters out afore now. They've been keeping their men on their home ranges for fear those gunmen of Bricklin's would try to pick 'em off one by one.' He pursed his lips. 'Those nesters don't know how lucky they are.'

While Hunter ate his meal the old doctor put him in the picture as regarded the valley and its occupants. The preacher listened carefully. It seemed that the governor had been right to send him here after all. A nasty little war was brewing, and there were too many sides for comfort.

Later Hunter saddled up and rode out of town. As he passed Herb Bricklin the young rancher struggled to his feet. His fetters jangled loudly.

'Ridin' out?' he sneered. 'That won't save your miserable hide. Pa's men'll get you sure.'

'Or vice versa,' Hunter said evenly. He touched his spurs to his horse's flanks and trotted down the street.

Bricklin's land lay mainly to the north and west of Antelope Wells, where the land was flatter and more fertile. His ranch was situated far down the valley, close to the river. The choice of site told Hunter that Bricklin had never even considered the possibility that he would have to defend the place. He had always expected to be the one doing the attacking.

The smaller ranchers had settled on the other side of town, where the land rose gently towards the distant mountains. Each man had built his ranch-house at the mouth of one of the canyons that branched off the main valley.

Hunter had examined the map of the region carefully before leaving the county seat, and knew that each canyon was watered by its own little stream. That gave the ranchers a secure water supply and a safe place to hold their cattle if the open valley exploded into war. There wouldn't be much in the way of grazing up there, but it would do at a pinch, for a week or two anyway.

The trail leading into the hills ran beside the river for the first few miles. Hunter had more savvy than to go that way. When he left the town limits he twitched the reins and directed his horse up the gentle slope away from the river and on to the rolling plain.

As he'd hoped, that caught Bricklin's watchers by surprise. As soon as they realized what he was doing two riders burst from a stand of cottonwoods beside the river and headed towards him at a gallop.

Hunter had no desire to make their closer acquaintance. He dug his heels into his horse's flanks. The big black gelding bunched his muscles and took off.

The gunmen's horses were good, but Hunter's was better and he slowly widened the gap between himself and his pursuers. The two gunmen lashed their horses unmercifully but gained no ground.

They drew their Winchesters from their scabbards and essayed a number of shots, but it is no easy thing to hit a moving target from the hurricane deck of a galloping horse, and they made no hits.

Soon Hunter and his two pursuers crossed the invisible border between the land claimed by Bricklin and the range occupied by the smaller ranchers. From this point on Bricklin's two men were in enemy territory. Go any further and they might get their heads shot off. Cursing, they gave up the chase and turned their horses' heads towards the town.

That suited Hunter. He wasn't looking for a gunbattle. If he never had to fire another shot in anger he would be a happy man. But it wasn't likely. Wherever he went there were evil men with guns in their hands. It seemed that God made sure he only went where there was fighting to do.

It was fair enough. Every person had his or her place in the great scheme of things. His was to be the sword of the Lord in the West. In any case, he had never killed anyone who wasn't better off dead.

Soon he was abreast of the mouth of a small valley that led off to his right. The range was dotted with cattle. Hunter estimated the herd was about two thousand strong. The rancher had driven his cows off the open range and on to the land he could protect. If the other small ranchers had done likewise it explained why he'd seen so few cows grazing on the open plain. But it wasn't a long-term solution to the problem. Two thousand cows would soon strip this little valley bare.

About a mile down the valley a small ranch-house sat on a low knoll. A thin column of smoke rose from its chimney. Barns and a long low bunkhouse stood nearby. Hunter pulled on the reins and brought his horse to a halt. He took a pair of battered field-glasses from one of his saddle-bags and examined the hillside up ahead. If the rancher had any sense he would have placed a man up there with a rifle to guard the mouth of the valley.

Sure enough, after scanning the hillside for a few minutes, Hunter saw a patch of blue lying between two large rocks. Probably a man's jean-clad leg, he decided. Not that it worried him. Even if the man had a Sharps Berdan sniper's rifle with a telescopic sight he couldn't reach Hunter from that position. The range was just too great. But if Hunter wanted to visit the Lazy J ranch he would have to come under the man's gun.

Well, he would just have to take the risk. Doc Thompson had assured him that Benjamin Teale wasn't the man to shoot a stranger down in cold blood or order it done, and he trusted the doctor's judgement. He put the field-glasses away and urged his horse up the gentle slope towards the house.

The man on the hillside got to his feet and fired three shots into the air. The sounds reverberated off the rocks and brought half a dozen men boiling out of the bunkhouse with guns in their hands. A moment later an old man came slowly out on to the ranch-house stoop on crutches. A woman was with him. Even at this distance Hunter could tell that she was young, blonde and pretty.

Hunter lifted his right hand into the air, palm forward in the sign of peace, and rode slowly up to the house.

Ignoring the guns that were being pointed his way by the men outside the bunkhouse he tipped his hat to the young woman, nodded to the elderly rancher and said: 'Good afternoon, Mr Teale. I'd like to talk to you, if I may.'

'You've got a hell of a nerve, ridin' in here

like this,' the man replied angrily, his white moustaches bristling. 'Well, I ain't like your boss. I don't pay dirty gunmen to shoot honest men down like dawgs. Say yer piece and then got off my ranch!'

Hunter smiled thinly. 'You've got hold of the wrong end of the stick, Teale. I don't work for Deke Bricklin.' He turned back his suitcoat and showed the marshal's badge pinned to his vest. 'I work for the people of Antelope Wells.' His smile broadened. 'And for God, of course, I'm also the new preacher in town.'

The old man's mouth fell open with surprise. There was a chorus of incredulous comment from his ranch-hands. The girl looked suspiciously at Hunter.

'Preachers don't fight,' she said bluntly. 'They don't think anyone else should, either, even when they're in the right. They always tell people like us to turn the other cheek. As if that'd do us any good!'

'I can see you've been unlucky with your preachers,' Hunter replied with a grin. 'There's no sin in resisting an evil man, and from what I've seen and heard Deke Bricklin definitely counts as an evil man.'

The old man snorted with laughter. 'He's got you there, girl.' He nodded at Hunter.

'Would you care to come inside, Mister Preacher? Maybe have a drink? If preachers do drink?'

Hunter knew when he was being baited. 'This one does,' he replied blandly, and swung down from his horse.

'Jake,' the old man called, 'look after this man's animal.'

Taking this as a signal, his men holstered their guns. One of them came forward, took the reins and led Hunter's horse away.

Hunter put out his hand and the old man took it. His grip was still powerful, despite his infirmity. 'I'm Benjamin Teale, and this is my granddaughter Amy.'

'Pleased to meet you. I'm Aaron Hunter,' the preacher replied in a friendly tone.

The girl still looked doubtfully at the black-clad stranger but the old man seemed to have made up his mind to listen to what he had to say. He led the way into the ranch-house, lowered himself carefully into a chair, laying his crutches on the floor beside him, told Hunter to sit himself down, and ordered the girl to pour them both a drink.

'So you've taken on the job of town marshal, have you?' he began. 'Think you can cut it?'

'With God's help, yes,' Hunter replied.

'He hasn't helped us much so far,' the girl burst out fiercely. 'Bricklin's men have already killed two of our riders. You're the marshal now, Mr Hunter. What are you going to do about it?'

Hunter was taken aback by her vehemence. 'There isn't anything much I can do,' he said regretfully. 'All the witnesses say your men drew first. They've got no reason to lie. They hate Bricklin and his men as much as you do, if not more.'

The girl's eyes flashed with anger. 'It was still murder, and you know it. Charlie and Laban were cowhands, not gunmen. Bricklin's hired killers didn't give them a chance.' She glared at Hunter. 'If you won't help us against Bricklin what good are you?'

She didn't give him a chance to reply, but rounded on her grandfather, saying bitterly, 'You can talk to this man if you want to, Grandpa, but I ain't staying to hear his lies. I'm going where the air don't smell of skunk.' She pushed rudely past Hunter and flounced out of the room, slamming the door behind her.

Her grandfather sighed heavily. 'Sorry about that, Marshal. Amy was very fond of old Laban Petter. He taught her to ride. If she was a man she'd be out huntin'

Bricklin's men and she cain't see why we ain't doin' it for her.'

Hunter took a sip of his whiskey. 'Their time will come, sooner or later. But I can understand how she feels. If it'll make her feel any better, you can tell her I've shot two of Bricklin's men already.'

The rancher's mouth fell open with surprise.

'And you can tell her that I'm holding Herb Bricklin in town as surety for his father's good behaviour.'

A huge grin split Benjamin Teale's face almost in two. 'You sure don't waste any time, do you, marshal?' he chuckled. 'Poor Amy. She was so sure you was scared o' Bricklin. Won't she be ashamed when she finds out she was wrong!'

'Tell her not to worry about it,' Hunter said easily. 'It was a natural mistake, under the circumstances. I wasn't offended in the least.'

'Maybe not,' chuckled the old man. 'But she'll be as mad as fire, just the same: with you, with me and with herself most of all.'

Hunter shrugged and changed the subject. 'Why haven't you ranchers got together long since and pinned Bricklin's ears back for him?'

The old man stroked his grizzled beard ruefully. 'Gettin' old, I guess. You see, we all came into this end of the valley more'n thirty years ago. Me, Joe Starr of the Bar S, Roman Hawkins of the Slash H, Ferdy Pratt of the F-P Connected, Mick Eaton of the Bar S and Andy Gorham of the Triangle.

'We drove a herd in here, divvied up the beeves, built ourselves ranch-houses and settled down to run cattle and live quiet. Some of us had wives already, and sent fer 'em to join us, the rest got married later. Most of us have got sons and daughters. Some of 'em married each other. Others brought in partners from outside. Four of us have got grandchildren.'

Hunter nodded understandingly. 'So this end of the valley is just one big family.'

'You got it.'

'If you stand up to Bricklin and someone gets killed, he's almost certain to be a relative.'

'That's right.'

'And the women don't want that.'

The old man sighed heavily. 'That's the problem, sure enough. Some of the young 'uns were all fer showing Deke Bricklin where he and his hired guns could get off, but the women soon put a stop to that. A man couldn't get any peace in his own house, the way their tongues was a flyin'.'

The memory made him scowl. Blackly. Hunter grinned behind his hand.

'They stopped cookin' our grub and swore they wouldn't go near a skillet until we gave our words we wouldn't go lookin' fer trouble,' the rancher added disgustedly.

'So how come your two riders went into Antelope Wells and got shot?' Hunter inquired.

The rancher shrugged. 'I guess they got fed up with stayin' home an' took a notion to go into town fer a drink or three. Old Laban was a salty old coot and as fer Charlie Dury, he was a mite too proud of his skill with his six-gun.

'Say,' he added suddenly. 'You must be pretty hot stuff with a gun your ownself, if'n you could take two o' Bricklin's men without gettin' a scratch!'

Hunter shrugged. 'The Lord was with me, I guess.'

The rancher was embarrassed. Was Hunter going to try to bring him to Jesus? That sort of thing was all right for women, but a man had better things to do with his time. He quickly changed the subject. 'So why did you ride out here?' he inquired.

'What can I do for you?'

'You've already done one of them,' replied Hunter, 'by pulling your cattle out of the valley. Your womenfolk were right about what would happen if you ranchers started fighting Bricklin. He's been recruiting gunmen from all over. Your men wouldn't stand a chance against them.' His lips tightened. 'I'll deal with Bricklin in my own good time.'

'I guess you will at that,' said Teale seriously. He had known men like Hunter before. Some of them had been lawmen, others were outlaws or gunfighters for hire, but they all had one thing in common: they did what they said they would do, or died in the attempt.

'Secondly, I want you and your friends to leave the nesters alone.'

Teale's face clouded over. 'Now, steady on, Mister,' he said coldly. 'I'm right grateful you're goin' to be fightin' our battles with Bricklin, but there's a limit, and you just crossed it. Bricklin may be a land-grabbin' swine but when all's said an' done he's a cattleman, same as us. He don't plough up the range an' he don't string wire across it.'

Teale brought his fist down on the arm of

his chair with a crash. 'I tells yer, Mister Marshal, if it weren't fer havin' ter keep lookin' over our shoulders fer Deke Bricklin and his gunnies we'd have run those damned nesters out o' the valley long since. If Deke goes ahead an' does it fer us we'll raise a glass to him and be glad to, even if we still tries our damnedest to shoot him out o' the saddle the next time we sees him.'

Hunter raised his eyes to heaven. 'What harm are the nesters doing? There's enough grazing land in the valley for everyone. And they've got a legal right to do what they've done. It's government land, remember. Anyone can file on it under the Homestead Act.'

Teale grasped his crutches and struggled to his feet. His face was hard.

'We came out here to get away from the damned government,' he grated out. 'We fought Indians and rustlers and dust-storms and locusts and made this land our home. We watered this land with our blood and our sweat. No one is going to take it away from us, law or no law.'

Hunter also got to his feet.

'I'm sorry you think that way,' he said regretfully. 'Because you're asking for trouble. Those farmers have rights under the law. As marshal, my duty is to uphold the law. If you take up arms against the farmers I'll be forced to fight you.'

'If you take sides with those dirty sodbusters against us ranchers ye'd better watch yer back, Mister Marshal,' the old man said angrily. 'We'll all be against yer then. Bricklin we can live with. Sodbusters never!'

Hunter's broadcloth-covered shoulders lifted and fell in a gesture of acceptance. 'I'd better go,' he said evenly. 'I'm doing no good here. I pray God will change your mind before it's too late.' He strode towards the door, then turned as a thought struck him.

'There'll be no more killing in Antelope Wells, now I'm marshal. So you and your friends can come to town to do your merchandising again.' Hunter grinned suddenly. 'The town needs your business. But you'll have to keep the peace, or take the consequences.'

'I'll tell 'em,' the old man grunted. 'Now git out o' here.'

FOUR

About mid-morning on the following day little Willy Kirkland came running up the street. Doc Thompson was sitting in a rocker outside his office, smoking a cigar.

'Hey, Willy!' he called. 'What's all the rush?'

The boy skidded to a halt. 'Where's Mister Hunter?' he gasped.

'Down to the old barn,' the doctor replied, gesturing with his cigar. 'Why...?'

But Willy was already on his way. Unknown to the townspeople, Hunter had recruited a number of their sons and daughters as his unofficial deputies. They were his eyes and ears in Antelope Wells. Children saw everything and heard everything and went largely unnoticed by the adults around them.

When Willy got to Hunter's new property the marshal was in his shirtsleeves, sweeping the floor. It was a big job. The floor of the barn was inches deep in musty old hay and horse dung. The rickety timber walls were festooned with dusty cobwebs.

Today was Friday. Service was on Sunday. Hunter knew he'd have to work hard if he was to get the barn ready in time.

Hunter straightened up with a groan as Willy raced into the barn. He was grateful for the interruption but wondered what was so urgent that it had brought the boy running all the way from his post at the southern end of town. He soon found out.

'Bricklins!' the boy gasped. 'Comin' this way! Lots of 'em!'

'Thank you, Willy,' Hunter said calmly. He had been expecting something of the kind. By all accounts Deke Bricklin wasn't the kind of man to leave his only son chained up for long.

Hunter leaned the broom against the wall, shrugged into his vest and suitcoat and slung his gunbelt round his waist. Now he was ready for anything.

When he came out of the barn he was met by a group of anxious townsmen. John Chapman had elected himself their spokes-person.

'What is it, marshal?' he asked.

'Riders. Coming this way,' Hunter replied shortly. 'Probably Deke Bricklin and his men.'

In the moment of silence that followed this statement Chapman exchanged glances with his fellow townsmen. First one man nodded, then the next, and the next. They would stand by their new marshal.

'We've all got guns, marshal. And with you to lead us we ain't afraid to use 'em,' Theodore Dardick, the fat, balding gunsmith, said courageously, and there was a murmur of agreement from the other men. 'What do you want us to do?'

Hunter smiled approvingly. He'd wondered whether the inhabitants of Antelope Wells would have the guts to back up their words with deeds. All too often in the past he'd had to face the forces of evil alone.

'Get your guns, find a good place to stand, and wait for my word,' he said. 'Bricklin thinks he's only got me to face. He doesn't realize he's bucking the whole town. I expect he'll back off when he sees your guns. Then I can talk to him. Maybe I can make him see sense.'

'Not on your life,' demurred old Doc Thompson. 'Deke Bricklin is a crazy man. He *knows* he's right. He won't listen to you or anyone.'

'Do you really think so?' Hunter said regretfully. He respected the old doctor's judgement. 'Maybe you're right. But I've got to try.'

'Of course you have. More blessed is the one sinner that repenteth, eh?' the doctor replied cynically. 'But keep your gun loose in your holster while you're talking to him, marshal, Bricklin ain't no gentleman. He'll throw down on you if you give him half a chance.'

'Then I won't give him one.' Hunter gathered all their eyes, 'We can end this thing now, if we stand together. Now get to your posts. And God go with you!'

When Deke Bricklin and his riders cantered into the town a few minutes later all the shop doors were shut and the sidewalks were deserted.

''S'like a ghost town,' one of the gunmen muttered to himself nervously. His saddle partner, a man of Irish extraction, hurriedly crossed himself. Their companions eyed the blank faces of the buildings uncertainly, their hands hovering over their guns. The whole set-up reeked of an ambush.

Outside the saloon a dishevelled figure struggled to his feet with a clanking of heavy iron chains.

'Pa!' he yelled hoarsely, 'Over here, Pa!'

Deke Bricklin held up a hand and his

gunmen reined in their horses.

'That you, boy?' the rancher called unbelievingly.

''Course it's me, Pa,' his son croaked. 'Get me out of here!'

The grizzled rancher dug his spurs into his horse's flanks and thundered down the street towards his son. The gunmen followed more closely. Some of them were smiling. They respected Deke Bricklin but despised his son. The rancher was a hard man, a killer like themselves. Herb Bricklin was a loud-mouth and a bully who traded on the fact that people were afraid of his father. More than likely he had a yellow streak running right up his back.

Deke Bricklin reined in so hard his horse's hindquarters almost touched the dusty street. He kicked his boots out of the stirrups, threw himself off its back and rushed to his son's side.

'Look Pa!' Herb held up his manacled arms and shook his chains angrily. 'Look what their bastard marshal done to me!'

The rancher's face went purple and the veins stood out on his forehead. How dare anyone treat him with such contempt? This insult could only be washed out with blood.

He spun round. His men instantly wiped

the smiles from their faces.

'Jase! Egan!' he commanded furiously. 'Go fetch that poxy blacksmith! I guess he made these here chains. Now he can damn well cut 'em off again.'

'OK, Boss,' the half-caste gunman called Egan Lonetree said obsequiously. He and his saddle partner began to back their horses away from the group of riders.

'An' be quick about it!' Bricklin added viciously. 'If'n my boy ain't free in five minutes we're burnin' the town.'

'Hold it right there!'

In the sudden silence Hunter pushed open the doors of the saloon and walked on to the sidewalk.

He made a striking figure. As always, he was dressed all in black but for his white shirt and the marshal's star gleaming silver on his vest. His suitcoat was folded back on the right side to allow him easy access to his holstered Colt .44. He held a Parker shotgun in his hands. The double click was loud in the silence as he eared back the hammers. At that range the two loads of buckshot would empty half a dozen saddles and they all knew it.

Some of Deke Bricklin's hired gunmen had seen the new marshal of Antelope Wells

74

at the funeral of their former comrades. Others were meeting him for the first time. But they all felt a shiver run down their spines at the sight of Hunter's black-clad figure. It made them think of lonely graves on a windswept Boot Hill somewhere, with a gibbous moon overhead and a whip-poorwill calling mournfully in the distance.

'Kill him, Pa!' cried Herb Bricklin, and directed a stream of foul language at the marshal of Antelope Wells.

'Shuddup, boy!' Deke Bricklin's voice was curt. Ignoring his son's angry splutterings he locked glances with the marshal.

Deke Bricklin was everything his son tried to be, but failed. Over forty years old now, he was still as strong as a longhorn bull and twice as vicious. A top hand with cattle, good with a gun, and as brave as a lion, he was utterly without scruple and had no respect for human life whatsoever. Originally from Missouri, he had ridden with Bloody Bill Anderson's band of cold-blooded murderers and looters during the War Between the States, and had come West at the war's end to put as much country as possible between him and some people who wanted to make him the guest of honour at a necktie party.

In the first years after the war thousands of unbranded cattle roamed wild over the plains. Deke Bricklin had quickly built a herd by branding everything he and his men could catch. Then he had driven the herd to Antelope Valley and settled down to live the life of a rancher.

A number of other men with similar ambitions had arrived at much the same time. Bricklin had tried to drive them out. He had failed. Now Antelope Valley was divided into two armed camps. Bricklin had the flat land on either side of the river to the north and west: the smaller ranchers had the side valleys to the south and east. The town of Antelope Wells was piggy in the middle.

Deke Bricklin had tried to get himself elected mayor of Antelope Wells. As mayor he would have been able to appoint a complaisant marshal, maybe a judge too. That would have put the other ranchers at a crippling disadvantage.

Bill Lonegan had ruined all that. But Lonegan was dead. So who was this stranger with the marshal's star on his chest? Could he be frightened off, or bought off? If not, he'd have to be killed, as Lonegan had been.

As his blue eyes clashed with the stranger's

76

cold grey ones Deke Bricklin realized that it wouldn't be so easy to kill this man. The new marshal of Antelope Wells looked as though he'd been there and done that, not once but many times.

'Who the hell are you?' the rancher growled.

'Hunter is the name,' the black-clad stranger replied easily. There was a twinkle in his eyes but his hands kept the shotgun aimed right at the rancher's brisket. 'I take it your name is Bricklin.'

'You're damn right it is,' the rancher said angrily. 'And that's my boy you've got there, chained up like a dog! What the hell do you do that for?'

'I'd got nowhere else to put him,' Hunter said with a derisive smile. 'This town hasn't got a jail-house. Not any more, anyway. It had one once, or so I'm told, but apparently it got burned down!'

Behind Deke Bricklin's back one or two of his gunmen sniggered quietly. The rancher went red in the face. This man was having fun at his expense. He struggled to control the fury mounting inside him.

'That's not an answer!' he bellowed. 'I asked you why you'd treated my son thisaway!'

The smile vanished from Hunter's eyes, leaving them looking like chips of ice. 'Your son tried to murder me. At a funeral, too.' His mouth twisted sardonically. 'Two of your men tried to kill me yesterday. It was them we were burying. You ought to be grateful, Mr Bricklin. Your son is still alive.'

'He tricked me, Pa!' Herb Bricklin protested. 'He had a hideout gun!'

'Shuddup, boy!' his father said contemptuously. 'You never seen the day you could outdraw a man like this'n.' He turned back to Hunter. 'You're goin' ter let him go?'

'No, I'm not,' Hunter replied evenly. 'He's a hostage for your good behaviour.'

'And what the hell does that mean?'

Hunter shrugged. 'Just what it says. You've been blockading the town, Bricklin. Making the other ranchers afraid to come in for supplies. Well ... that's got to stop.'

'And who's going to make me? You?'

'If I have to,' Hunter said calmly. 'But I hope you'll see sense. This valley is big enough for everyone.'

'This valley is mine!' Bricklin said furiously, and made a sweeping gesture that embraced the whole town. 'So's the town. Hell, it's built on my land, ain't it? Don't that make it mine? O' course it does.'

'The townspeople don't seem to think so,' Hunter said mildly. 'They voted me in as marshal. As mayor, too.'

'They can vote all they likes,' Bricklin replied angrily, 'but their votes ain't worth a hill o' beans. Not while I've got the guns, they ain't.'

'But *have* you got the guns, Mr Bricklin?' Hunter raised his voice and called, 'It's time!'

The batwing doors of the saloon swung open and Curly Watts came out on to the stoop. He held the sawn-off shotgun that normally lived on a shelf under the bar. Rio Harkness came out after him, six-guns at the ready, and broke left. Rosey and another man Hunter didn't yet know by name followed Rio and moved to the right.

Down the street John Chapman stepped from the doorway of the general store, a Winchester in his hands. The click as he worked the lever to jack a shell into the breech was loud in the sudden silence. On the other side of the street more gunbarrels suddenly appeared at the open windows of the doctor's office and the saddlery. Standing in the doorway of the carpenter's shop whiskery old Jim Bacher lined up his ancient Hawken rifle on Bricklin's redshirted chest. More armed men popped up from all over.

The rancher and his band of hired gunmen were caught totally off balance. Their hands were on their reins, not hovering over their holsters. Some flushed with anger, others went white with sudden fear, but they all stayed as still as mice. One wrong move and they would be blown to doll rags.

Deke Bricklin swelled with rage as he looked at the gun-toting townsmen. Somehow this black-clad stranger had turned these bleating sheep into ravening wolves. Part of him wanted to pull out his gun and start blasting. But he had more sense than to give in to the temptation. Right now the odds were against him. Tomorrow was another day.

'Mighty brave, ain't they now they've got a *man* to lead them,' he sneered, then turned his burning eyes on Hunter. 'OK, marshal. You win, *this* time. Now what?'

'You ride away,' the marshal said evenly. 'And leave this town alone in future. The other ranchers, too. As I said, this valley is big enough for everyone.'

'And if I don't?'

Hunter's voice hardened. 'To quote from

the Book of Deuteronomy Chapter 30 Verse 19: "I call heaven and earth to record this day against you, that I have set before you life and death, blessing and cursing: therefore choose life, that both thou and thy seed may live".'

Deke Bricklin clenched his fists. The Bible puncher *was* laughing at him. But what the hell could he do? The townsmen had the drop on him and his men. If he pulled a gun on the marshal he'd be blasted out of the saddle a split-second later. But he couldn't just ride away and leave this man to his triumph, he really couldn't.

He kicked his feet out of his stirrups and swung down off his horse. 'Think you're mighty clever, don't you, Preacher?' he spat. 'Mighty brave too, with all these guns to back ye up. Are ye brave enuff ter settle this thing man ter man? No guns, mind you: just good old-fashioned knuckle and skull fightin'.'

In making this offer Bricklin thought he was on to a damn good each-way bet. He was three inches taller than the marshal and outweighed him by at least forty pounds. His fists were like hams and his knuckles were hardened by more than a hundred fights. He had never yet met the man he couldn't beat. He had no doubt that given the chance he could hammer the marshal into the ground.

He fully expected the marshal to turn his offer down flat. Gunmen rarely fought with their fists. They had too much to lose. A broken finger often healed crookedly, and a crooked finger could ruin a man's draw.

But the townsmen wouldn't know that. All they would see was that their new marshal was afraid to meet his enemy's challenge. That would diminish the man in the eyes of his supporters and shake their confidence in his leadership.

'Well?' he drawled insolently. 'Are ye man enuff ter face me without yer guns?'

'"This day will the Lord deliver thee into mine hand, and I shall smite thee",' the marshal replied confidently, tossing his shotgun to Rio Harkness and slipping out of his coat.

Deke Bricklin unfastened his gunbelt and hung it over his saddle horn. Hunter un-buckled his own gunbelt and handed it and his coat to Curly Watts, then stepped down into the street.

The two men circled around each other cautiously. Bricklin was the first to attack. He lunged forward and swung a roundhouse right. Hunter ducked under it and slipped inside the big man's guard, rattling Bricklin's ribs with a flurry of lefts and rights.

Bricklin didn't even seem to notice the blows. His mighty arms closed round Hunter's chest and tightened like a vice. Hunter's arms were crushed against his sides.

'I'm gonna kill you, marshal,' the big man grunted and increased the pressure until Hunter felt his ribs creaking. He jerked his knee up into Bricklin's groin. The big man had been expecting it and swivelled to take the blow on his thigh.

Hunter was already finding it difficult to breathe. Bright lights were flashing in front of his eyes. If he couldn't break Bricklin's grip soon he was done for.

He could faintly hear the rancher's gunmen shouting encouragement to their boss. His own supporters were ominously silent. It was time for drastic measures. He jerked his head forward viciously and the rancher's beaky nose exploded in a shower of blood. Hunter repeated the action again and again until he felt the arms round his chest begin to weaken. He jerked backwards and broke the big man's grip.

The two men staggered apart. Hunter's chest was heaving and his lungs were wheezing like a blacksmith's bellows. He leaned forward and rested his hands on his knees while he struggled for breath. His chest was on fire and he was sure he must have got at least one cracked rib.

Bricklin acknowledged the cheers of his supporters with a wave of a meaty fist, then unfastened his bandanna and wiped the blood from his face. His nose felt twice its normal size and hurt like the devil. But he could see that he had hurt Hunter just as much, if not more. He tossed the bandanna aside and came forward, fists cocked and ready.

Hunter straightened up with an effort. Their first clash had taught him that if he allowed Bricklin to fight rough-house style he was bound to lose. The rancher had a grip like a grizzly bear!

As Bricklin shuffled ponderously towards him the marshal took a step to the rear, then another and another. His caution was greeted with jeers by the rancher's employees. Deke Bricklin came after him, grinning contemptuously.

Suddenly Hunter seemed to trip, and stumble. Seizing his chance, Bricklin plunged after him, fists whirling. But it was all a feint. Recovering his footing as if by magic, Hunter sidestepped the rancher's clumsy rush and clipped him hard on the ear as he went by. The fleshy organ split under the blow and a stream of red began to flow down the big man's bristly cheek.

But he was far from done yet. Whipping round with amazing speed he crashed a powerful left into Hunter's damaged ribs. The preacher folded over the blow as his breath left him in an explosive *whoof* of agony. A second later a right to the jaw straightened him up again. His reply rattled Bricklin's teeth for him and knocked him back a pace.

There was a brief pause while they took a quick breath and then they both came boring in again. Toe to toe they slugged at each other amid the cries of encouragement from their supporters. Hunter tucked his head against the big man's cowhide vest and pounded his belly with a flurry of lefts and rights until the rancher felt as though he was being broken in half.

Bricklin hammered at Hunter's bruised ribs for a while without bothering the preacher too much but when he shifted his target to Hunter's kidneys the preacher threw him off and mashed his lips with a long left as he staggered backwards.

Hunter followed up swiftly but Bricklin wasn't as damaged as he seemed. He caught the marshal in a rolling hip-lock and threw him to the hard-packed and by now blood-flecked sand.

Hunter's head hit the ground with enough force to partially stun him. For a moment or two he lay there shaking his head in an effort to clear it.

Deke Bricklin grinned evilly and took a mighty kick at Hunter's head with his heavy boot. If the blow had landed it would have ended the fight then and there. It might even have killed him. Not that Bricklin would have cared if it did. He had always meant to stomp the interfering stranger to death if he could.

At the last moment Hunter rolled aside and the swinging boot missed his head. For a moment Bricklin was off-balance. Hunter grabbed the man's ankle and heaved and Bricklin came crashing down to the ground.

He was a heavy man and the fall drove all the breath from his body. When he finally got to his feet the marshal was ready for him. Hunter stepped in close and drove a left and a right into the big man's solar plexus. They hit with the force of a pile-driver and stopped Bricklin dead in his tracks.

Then Hunter put all his remaining strength into a right hook. It hit the big man's chin like a thunderbolt. The crack of breaking bone was clearly heard over the shouts of the two fighters' partisans. Bricklin's eyes crossed, he swayed briefly from side to side, then he fell backwards into the dirt, out cold.

Herb Bricklin gave a cry of desolation and despair. His father had never been beaten before. The gunmen were silent, though a few of them cast admiring glances Hunter's way. Even these hired killers could appreciate a well-fought fight and give due credit to the winner. The townsmen shouted themselves hoarse, praising Hunter and lauding his courage and skill to the skies.

His chest heaving, Hunter turned to face Bricklin's men.

'Show's over, boys,' he gasped through his spilt and bleeding lips. 'Put your boss on his horse and take him home. His son stays here.'

Ben Strutt urged his horse a pace in front of the other Bricklin riders. He kept his hands well clear of his guns.

'We'll do like you say, marshal. I guess you've earned the right to give the orders, fer today, at least.' His mouth twisted. 'But you ain't seen the last of us, not by a long chalk you ain't.'

'"Sufficient unto the day is the evil thereof",' Hunter replied sardonically. 'Now, get going!'

He turned his back on Strutt and the other men and staggered towards the saloon amid the plaudits of the crowed. Taking a bandanna from his pants pocket he wiped the worst of the blood from his bruised and beaten face.

Curly Watts offered him his gunbelt. He took it and belted it on, then slowly and painfully donned his suitcoat. Finally he clapped his hat on his head.

Two of Bricklin's men hoisted their semi-conscious employer on to his horse, and with Ben Strutt leading the way they all rode slowly out of town.

Hunter pushed through the batwing doors of the saloon and slumped into the nearest chair. The exultant townsmen poured in after him. They were feeling mighty proud of themselves. With Hunter to lead them they had stood up to Bricklin and his gunnies and made them back down. Now they aimed to celebrate.

More than that, they had seen their new marshal destroy Big Deke Bricklin with his fists in a fight that would be remembered in Antelope Wells for a generation. They crowded round the battered and exhausted Hunter and praised him to the skies.

It was a long time before their enthusiasm began to wane and the weary marshal could make his escape. Aching in every limb he lurched down the street to the hotel, into which he had moved his things earlier that day, dragged himself painfully up the stairs, then fell on to his bed fully dressed. In less than five seconds he was asleep.

FIVE

After breakfast the next day Hunter climbed on to the roof of his new property and scanned the country with his field-glasses. Were Bricklin's men still blockading the town, or had the sentries been withdrawn?

Half an hour later he decided that either Bricklin had pulled his men back to the ranch or they were better Indians than he had thought they were.

He descended from his lofty perch, saddled his horse and rode out of town. As promised, he was going to pay a call on the nesters. But first he aimed to survey the area. He turned his horse's head towards the high hills and kicked it into a trot.

For a mile or two the ground rose smoothly. The grass was green and rich. Insects buzzed and hummed in the undergrowth. Birds sang far overhead in the clear blue sky. This was prime cattle-country.

Then the land became more broken. Large lumps of craggy rock poked through the grass, which grew scrubby and thin and eventually petered out altogether. Rattle-snakes sunned themselves on flat rocks, slithering away as Hunter got close. A buzzard wheeled lazily overhead.

Hunter's horse picked its way cautiously over flat slabs of rock in which shards and splinters of mica glistened in the sunlight. The ground grew steeper and steeper until Hunter was forced to dismount and lead his horse by its bridle. He was dripping with sweat by the time he reached the crest.

The view was worth the climb. From this vantage point he could see the whole valley laid out before him like a sand-lot model. The town of Antelope Wells was off to his left. At this distance the houses looked like toys. Further to his left a thin column of smoke rising from this side of the valley showed him where the Bricklin ranch-house was situated. On his right, other columns of smoke indicated the locations of the smaller ranches.

One trail came up the valley, passed through Antelope Wells, and went on up into the hills. The other entered the valley through a notch in the rimrock to the east, crossed the river, ran through the town, and disappeared over the crest on the western side of the valley. Hunter had come that way from Piute Crossing.

The course of the river that flowed down the valley was lined with cottonwood trees. Between the trees Hunter could see a wide expanse of sandy river bed and the faint glistening of light on water. The river was low and getting lower.

The nesters had settled on the far bank of the river. They had built their sod huts on a bench well above the water. All round their huts the land had been torn up by the plough. Piles of larch poles and coils of sparkling new wire made it clear that they were planning to fence off their croplands.

Hunter smiled grimly to himself. These nesters were squatting on the best land in the valley. They were also blocking the ranchers' access to this side of the river. Right now there was plenty of water in the streams that flowed through the ranchers' home ranges, but when the dry weather came and the little streams dried up the ranchers would be wanting to drive their cattle down to the river to drink, and then God help the squatters!

Up here on the caprock the land was flat and bare, with occasional tufts of spiny cactus and other plants that could live without much in the way of water. There was hardly any cover, so there was no real chance of an ambush. Nevertheless, Hunter kept his Winchester in his hands and his finger on the trigger just in case of trouble.

The heat reflected from the bare rock at man and horse with unremitting fury. Hunter told himself that he was a fool for coming up here. At the same time he knew that he had been right to do so. Looking at a map was one thing, listening to a man describing the shape of the country was better still, but there is nothing to beat seeing the lie of the land for yourself.

As the morning wore on and the sun climbed higher and higher into the sky Hunter made his weary way round the head of the valley. As the map had indicated, six tributary streams rose under the caprock and flowed down to form the river that flowed past Antelope Wells. Six times he dismounted and raked these little valleys through his field-glasses. They were all thronged with beeves. He could see the tiny figures of men on horseback riding around down there too. Each valley was home to a small ranch-house and associated out-buildings.

It seemed that Benjamin Teale had told him the truth. The six smaller ranchers were doing their best to stay out of trouble. But it couldn't last for ever. That number of cattle would strip these narrow canyons bare in a week or two. Then the ranchers would have to drive theiir cattle back on to the open range or watch them die of starvation.

Hunter's lips tightened. He had a week, two at the most, to sort things out before guns started blazing in Antelope Valley. Would Bricklin draw in his horns? Not if his son was anything to go by, he wouldn't.

Sighing for the folly of men, he kicked his horse into a trot and leaving the head of the valley behind, headed north.

The terrain was different here, on the eastern side of the valley. Instead of bare granite, glinting with chips of mica and veins of yellow quartz, the rock was soft sandstone, weathered into fantastic shapes by wind and water. There were a thousand places for a man to hide hereabouts, and Hunter stopped repeatedly and raked the twisted rocks ahead of him with his field-glasses before moving on again.

But he saw no one, and no one took a shot at him.

When Hunter came down off the rim without having seen a soul he began to relax his vigilance somewhat. He was hot and sweaty and his horse was tired. Both of them were hungry too. Hunter's big black gelding kept trying to grab a mouthful of greenery from the bushes as they threaded their way through the jumbled rocks and stands of spindly larches at the foot of the rim.

Eventually he came out on to the valley floor. A couple of miles ahead of him was the river and its screen of cottonwood trees. Soon he would hear the splash of water and the sighing of the gentle breeze in the broad green leaves. He longed to bathe his face in the cool waters of the river.

But first he had to make a call on the nesters.

One of their rough cabins was sited directly between him and the river. The others were spaced out at intervals along the same level stretch of ground, Hunter smiled sourly. They had chosen well. From the look of the lush grass underfoot the land was fertile, and they had built their houses well above the highest point the river ever reached in floodtime. The nesters must have thought they had reached the Promised Land, a place where they could raise crops and a family in peace and prosperity.

There was only one problem. The ranchers!

As Hunter rode towards the nearest cabin he noticed a row of marker poles half-way between it and the next one. He had warned Benjamin Teale that these men were entitled to file on unclaimed government land under the Homestead Act, and it seemed that they had already gone and done it. There was no way the ranchers could get them out now, not legally, anyway.

The boom of a heavy rifle and the sound of tearing cloth as a bullet passed overhead was Hunter's first warning that his approach had not passed unnoticed. His horse shied nervously, but he was not disturbed. The shot had not been aimed to kill.

Hunter stood up in his stirrups and waved his hat over his head to show that he was coming in peace.

A burly, unshaven man in dungarees and flat-heeled boots came out of the door and stood glowering at the approaching Hunter. He held a Ballard single-shot rifle in his hands. The weapon was out of date in this age of repeating carbines, but in experienced hands it was still deadly. And this man, farmer or no, looked hard as nails and grimly determined to hold on to what he had got.

A faint sound made Hunter's eyes flick

quickly to the open window of the soddy. The barrel of a pre-war Colt Dragoon cap-and-ball pistol was pointing in his direction. Hunter pretended he hadn't noticed.

'Good morning,' he began politely. 'My name is Hunter.'

'I don't care what your name is,' the nester said gruffly, 'What do you want?'

'I'm the new marshal in Antelope Wells,' Hunter said calmly, turning back his coat so that the man could see his badge.

'Appointed by the cattlemen, I dare say,' the farmer said cynically. 'Well, that don't cut no ice with us. This ain't Antelope Wells, and we ain't moving.'

'Whoever said you were?' Hunter replied evenly.

That took the farmer by surprise. 'I thought you'd come to tell us to quit,' he said.

'On the contrary,' replied Hunter, the ghost of a smile touching his lips. 'I was elected by the townspeople. They've had enough of being pushed around Deke Bricklin and his ilk. They're making a new start. I've come to let you know that you and your friends are welcome in town from now on.'

The farmer read truth in the saturnine

stranger's level gaze. His rifle barrel drooped as he turned his head. 'Did you hear that, mother?' he bawled.

A stout, red-faced woman appeared in the doorway of the soddy. A Colt Dragoon pistol hung forgotten from her work-roughened hand. 'Of course I did, you old fool,' she said affectionately. 'I ain't deaf.'

She spoke to Hunter. 'You look like a good man, Mr Hunter. Will ye get down of'n that horse and take a bite to eat with us?'

'I'd be glad to,' Hunter replied eagerly. His belly rumbled loudly to give point to his words.

The woman laughed. 'That ain't no lie, anyways. There's water fer washin' round the back. Jake, you better wash up too.'

'OK, mother,' her husband replied.

'What about my horse?' Hunter inquired, kicking his feet out of the stirrups and swinging down from the saddle.

'Eli'll care fer him,' the nester replied, his lips twitching beneath his walrus moustache. 'Eli, you come out here right now an' take the man's horse.'

A stocky young man of eighteen or so came out of the door. He was holding another Ballard.

'Yes Pa,' he said brusquely, nodded to

Hunter, man to man, and led Hunter's big gelding away.

Hunter looked quizzically at the nester. 'Got any more gunfighters in there?'

The man grinned broadly. 'Ruth, Becca, Zack! Come out an' meet our guest.'

There was a scuffling inside the house and a muffled scream, then two girls aged about sixteen and fourteen came shyly through the door. Each girl held a pistol, a Walch Navy .36. They were followed by a boy of about ten or eleven. He was carrying a Kentucky rifle a foot taller than he was.

Hunter bowed gravely to the two girls, winked at the boy, then turned his satirical gaze on their father.

'Cautious sort of man, aren't you?' he said.

'Maybe that's why I'm still alive,' the man replied with a smile. 'Got the habit fightin' Injuns. In the Army, that was. Never thought I'd need to be that way out here though. Seems I was wrong. Nesters ain't too popular round here. Not with the ranchers, anyways.'

His wife broke in impatiently. 'Stow your gab, Jake Morrison, an' show the man where he can wash up. You can do all the talkin' you've had a mind to over the dinner table.'

The nester locked eyes with Hunter. 'You married, marshal?'

'No.'

'Wise man.'

'And who's gonna get the burnt bits from the bottom of the pot?' his wife cackled, putting her arms round her three youngest children.

'Pa is!' they chorused happily.

The woman shepherded her young ones into the house, pausing only to add over her shoulder: 'I'd git washin', if I was you, Jake Morrison. The longer ye take, the more burnt it'll get.'

The nester grinned at Hunter. 'That there's a woman to ride the river with. You get one like that, marshal, an' you'll be doin' all right. Come on, you heard her, let's get cleaned up.'

He turned away without noticing the look of pain that swept fleetingly across Aaron Hunter's face. The marshal's wife was long dead, but her memory was still fresh in his mind.

Hunter was impressed by the interior of the soddy. The beaten earth floor had been swept clear and then incised with a floral pattern that must have been copied from an illustration of a carpet in Godey's Lady's

Book. The table and chairs were better made than most. There were bright chintz curtains at the windows and there was a matching cloth on the table. Mrs Morrison had obviously done her best to turn this rough hut into a proper home.

The West needs people like this, willing to work hard and put down roots, thought Hunter approvingly. He could sympathize with the cattlemen though. They had tamed this land and thought that gave them a right to hold it for ever. But nothing remained the same for long, and the day of the old-style rancher was almost done. These nesters were the vanguard of the future. The ranchers would have to adapt, or go under.

No doubt some of them would try to hold back the future with their roaring six-guns. But not in Antelope Valley. Not if Hunter could help it.

When Hunter and the Morrisons were all seated round the table Hunter said: 'As well as being marshal, I'm also a preacher. Would you care for me to say grace?'

Morrison's bushy eyebrows shot up. 'You're pullin' my leg, ain't yer?' he queried. His wife and children eyed their guest with disbelief. He was dressed like a preacher, sure enough, but he was also packing a Colt and a Bowie. They'd never seen a preacher armed that way before.

'I'm a preacher by vocation,' their dinner guest confirmed with a smile, 'marshal only by necessity. Oh, yes. I'm mayor too. Antelope Wells is so small that one man can do all three jobs.'

'Well, I'll be...' Jacob Morrison began incredulously, but his wife promptly cut him off.

'You watch your mouth, Jake Morrison.' She turned to Hunter. 'We'd surely admire for you to say grace, Mr Hunter.'

The Morrison family bowed their heads as Hunter gave thanks to God for the food they were about to eat. Then Mrs Morrison removed the lid of the stew-pot. A glorious smell came out. She ladled a generous portion of stew on to Hunter's plate, then served the others.

Hunter raised his spoon to his lips. The stew was good, damned good. He cocked an eye at Morrison's eldest son, who was looking pleased with himself despite his efforts to hide it.

'Antelope, eh? Did you get him, boy?'

'Yes sir,' Eli replied proudly. 'That Ballard of mine may be a mite old, but it's a straight-shootin' gun.'

'It's the man behind the gun that counts,' Hunter replied approvingly, and Eli went beet-red with pleasure. His sisters exchanged glances and giggled softly behind their hands.

'I'm a good shot too,' piped up young Zack.

'Speak when you're spoken to, boy,' his father said sternly and pretended to cuff him into silence, his hand ruffling the boy's hair affectionately.

When the meal was over Hunter and Morrison went outside for a companionable smoke.

'You've a fine family, Mr Morrison,' said Hunter. There was a faintly wistful note in his voice. 'The kind this country needs if it is going to grow. And from what you tell me I gather the other families are much the same.' His voice hardened suddenly. 'So why did you and your friends settle just here? Can't you see you're blocking the ranchers' access to the river?'

'We can now!' Morrison said defensively. 'But we sure as hell didn't know it when we filed our claims back in the county seat. The land agent there just showed us a map of the valley and told us to pick our spots. Then it was up to us to get here with our gear and prove up our claim. That meant buildin' a soddy and breakin' the ground for a crop as soon as ever we could. It wasn't until a bunch of riders showed up an' tol' us to get out or be killed that we had any idea we was squatting on someone else's range.'

He shrugged his heavy shoulders. 'By then it was too late ter move, even if we wanted to. Each family had built itself a soddy and ploughed an acre o' ground. None of us were about to up stakes and move on the say-so of a bunch of gunnies. An' we'd paid the land agent good money to register our claim to this ground. We wouldn't get that back in a hurry, now would we, marshal?'

Hunter shook his head. 'I guess not.'

'There you are then,' Morrison said defiantly. 'If those ranchers want to get us out o' here they'll have ter do it the hard way. With guns! They think it'll be easy. They're professionals an' we're only a bunch o' farmers. What they don't know is, most of us fought fer the Union in the late difficulty, an' we've all got guns and are ready and willin' ter use 'em.'

Hunter shook his head sadly. It seemed that the Devil had got into everyone in Antelope Valley and made them eager for a fight.

'What about your families?' he asked. 'What do they think about it?'

'They knew the risks we was takin', comin' out here,' Morrison replied firmly. 'They'll stand by us.'

Hunter gave up. 'Well, we must just hope it won't come to that,' he said with resignation. 'Anyway, I must be on my way.'

'Eli! Bring the marshal's horse,' Morrison called. He put out his hand. 'You're a good man, marshal. I know you don't want any fightin'. Nor do I.' His voice hardened. 'But if those ranchers don't leave us alone there'll be blood spilt.'

Hunter took the other man's work-roughened hand and shook it firmly. 'It's my job to make sure it doesn't come to that,' he said grimly. 'Don't forget that you and your friends are welcome to come into town whenever you want to. Why not come to service on Sunday? We start at ten o' clock.'

Before Morrison could reply his wife put her head out of the open window and said with a broad grin: 'We'll be there Mr!' Her head disappeared before Morrison or Hunter could make a reply.

Morrison gave Hunter a look of amused resignation. 'You heard the boss,' he growled. 'We'll be there.'

Hunter swung himself into the saddle. 'Good,' said he. 'Thanks for the meal.'

'Our pleasure.'

Hunter kicked his horse into motion and rode away.

SIX

Riding easily, Hunter reached the ford in less than five minutes. But he made no effort to cross the slowly moving stream. He had seen a plume of dust rising in the distance. He pulled out his field-glasses and watched it for a minute or two until he was sure it was heading his way.

That plume of dust means trouble, he thought glumly. It'd take a big band of riders to raise that much dust. And there was only one reason for them to be coming this way. To attack the nesters.

Hunter put his field-glasses away in his saddle-bag, turned his horse and headed back the way he'd come. There was still time to warn the nesters that trouble was coming their way.

When Hunter rode up in a cloud of dust Jake Morrison was busy chopping at an old tree stump in the dooryard. The nester sank the axe into the battered stump and left it there.

'You're back mighty quick, Marshal,' he

commented dryly.

'With good reason,' replied Hunter. 'There's a band of riders coming this way. Of course they *may* be aiming to make a social call, but I doubt it.'

'You think they're aimin' to throw us of'n this place?' Morrison said with dismay.

Hunter shrugged. 'Seems likely. If I were you, I'd get inside the house. They'll be here soon enough.'

'What about my neighbours?' protested Morrison. 'Hadn't we better warn them too?'

'Your place is nearest the ford, Morrison, so I guess those riders will be coming here first. If there's trouble your friends'll hear the shooting, sure enough. But you could send that young son of yours to warn them if you like.'

He swung down out of the saddle and led his horse into Morrison's lean-to stable. He tied it up, then slid his Winchester from its boot and tucked it under his arm.

'I guess that means you're stayin' to help us,' the farmer said gratefully.

'Of course,' replied Hunter soberly. 'That's my job.'

He was expecting to have to face Deke Bricklin's gunmen. But when the riders got closer he was surprised to recognize some of the men he'd seen at Teale's ranch when he'd ridden out there the day before.

He wasn't to know that after he'd gone the old rancher had summoned his friends to a meeting and given them the news that the new marshal of Antelope Wells was a nester-lover.

The ranchers had agreed to push the nesters out of Antelope Valley right away, before the new marshal of Antelope Wells could do something to stop them. Twenty men ought to be enough to do the job, they thought, and made up a posse of their best and most gun-handy men, led by Joe Starr, the leathery owner of the Bar S.

Joe was in his fifties, too old and canny to take any pleasure in shooting scrapes. But, like all the other ranchers, he hated nesters. When he had come West in the early 1850s a man could ride for a week without seeing a fence, and he was determined to keep it that way. No damned nesters would start stringing wire across the open range while he was still alive to prevent it!

He aimed to give Morrison a good beating, stand by while he and his family loaded their meagre possessions on to their wagon and send them on their way. Then they were to pull down his fences and rip the roof off his soddy.

If the other nesters didn't get the message and start to move out he and his men were going to wreck another farm, and another, and another, until the nesters had all been driven out.

Most of the cowboys he had brought with him were young men, full of piss and vinegar and spoiling for a fight. They were itching to go head to head with Deke Bricklin and his band of hired gunnies, and bitterly resented the fact that their bosses had ordered them to stay out of town in an effort to keep them out of trouble.

They had eagerly agreed to join Joe's posse. Hazing sodbusters wasn't anywhere near as good as starting a war with Deke Bricklin and his gunnies, but it was better than nothing. But they hadn't expected to have to draw their guns, let alone use them. These were *nesters* for God's sake, not *real* western men.

These nesters looked full of fight, though. Their soddy had been built like a fortress. Its door and shutters were pierced with loopholes and half a dozen guns were pointing their way.

Even so, they thought, the job still had to

be done. They had made their brags and weren't about to ride home again without even firing a shot. If they did that the womenfolk would laugh at them. More importantly, each man would wonder in his heart of hearts whether he had been glad of the excuse not to fight. This fear of seeming less than a man would drive them on to kill and die.

Joe Starr was more sensible. He might have hated nesters, but he knew a stacked deck when he saw one. These nesters had been tipped off and were ready for them. If he launched an attack on the soddy a lot of his men would die. But there were more ways than one of skinning a cat. Maybe he could persuade them to leave the valley without a fight.

'Hello, the house,' he called. 'I wanna talk.'

The front door opened and Morrison stepped out on to the stoop, his Ballard resting in the crook of his arm. He looked tough and determined.

'What do you want?' he growled.

'You to up stakes and move on,' Joe Starr replied harshly. 'This is all open range round here. No room for sodbusters.'

'This is my land, deeded and filed,' Morrison said determinedly. 'You're the one who's trespassing, not me!'

There was a growl of anger from the men with Joe Starr. One of the young men from the Slash H swung his rifle up. The man beside him, older and more sensible, promptly knocked it down again.

Joe Starr twisted round in his saddle. 'The next man who lays a hand on his gun can go straight back to his ranch and draw his time,' he said coldly.

He turned back to face the burly sod-buster. 'We ain't unreasonable men,' he said. 'So we'll give you a week to get out. And as I can see you've put a lot of work into this place I'll give you fifty dollars to boot.'

Morrison went red. 'You know what you can do with your fifty dollars...' he shouted angrily, and took a step towards the leathery rancher.

'Morrison!'

The door to the soddy opened and Hunter stepped out. The snap in his voice halted the farmer in his tracks. Morrison glanced at the marshal, flushed, and retreated to the stoop.

'That's the man who came to see the boss,' blurted one of the men from the Lazy J. 'He's the new marshal of Antelope Wells.'

114

'That's right,' Hunter confirmed, turning back the edge of his coat so that they could all see his badge. 'And I won't have any fighting on my patch. These farmers have a legal right to the land, and I'm here to make sure they don't get driven off by anyone. Why don't you fellers ride on back where you came from and leave this man and his family in peace?'

Joe Starr glared at the black-clad stranger. 'You ain't got no authority out here,' he grated. 'That badge stops workin' at the edge of town!'

Hunter smiled tautly. 'This one doesn't!' He felt in a pocket of his vest and brought out another badge. The rays of the afternoon sun turned it to gold as he held it up.

'A deputy US marshal!' blurted one of the men behind Joe Starr amid a chorus of curses and groans from his companions.

The rancher scowled blackly. That badge gave the stranger all the authority he needed. Government law had come to Antelope Valley.

Joe Starr knew he had a difficult decision to make. If he and his men killed the stranger, and from the look of him that wouldn't be an easy job, sooner or later another US marshal would come to the valley and he would have to answer for the crime. There were far too few US marshals to police the whole West, but there was one thing they never gave up on, and that was avenging their murdered fellow marshals.

That meant he'd have to kill all the nesters, including their women and children, as well as the marshal. He couldn't afford to leave any witnesses to the crime.

The grisly thought made the rancher blench. In his time he'd fought Indians and rustlers and was resigned to the necessity of sooner or later fighting Deke Bricklin and his gunmen. But he'd never killed a woman or a child and he wasn't about to start now. And that went for the men with him too.

But if he rode away now, it meant that he was accepting the nesters' right to the land they had taken. Would his fellow ranchers accept that?

He shrugged his thin shoulders. It looked like they'd have to. It was either that or kill the stranger and massacre all the nesters. And somehow he couldn't see his fellow ranchers agreeing to do that!

'OK. You win,' he said reluctantly, ignoring the cries of protest from the younger and more foolish cowboys behind him. 'I cain't speak fer all the other ranchers, but I guess they'll have to swaller it too. We'll leave 'em alone.'

'Good man,' Hunter said approvingly. He turned to the astonished Morrison. 'When you get round to putting up your fences you'll be sure to leave a way down to the river for these men's cattle, won't you.'

It wasn't a question.

Morrison was taken aback. He scratched his bristly chin in thought for a moment. Then he stepped forward and offered his hand to the leader of the cowboys.

'I guess I will at that,' he said with a reluctant grin. 'Shake on it, Mister?'

Joe Starr leaned down from the saddle and took the sodbuster's work-gnarled hand.

'Deal,' he said laconically.

The door of the soddy opened and Mrs Morrison came out, the heavy Colt Dragoon cap-and-ball pistol drooping from her hand. She was followed by the other four members of the family. Like her they were each carrying a weapon.

A couple of sod-busters stepped out from behind a clump of bushes two hundred yards away. Each man was carrying a Springfield rifle. More armed men and boys popped up from all over.

Joe Starr's cowboys hadn't realized what

an army they had been facing. If their leader hadn't decided to make peace some of them would have been killed for sure.

Joe Starr raised his bushy eyebrows. 'Seems like I done the right thing,' he drawled.

Jake Morrison's mouth twitched under his heavy moustache. 'Us farmers stand by each other,' he declared. 'Stand by our friends, too. I trust we're goin' ter be friends?'

Joe Starr laughed. 'I sure wouldn't like ter be yer enemy, Mr Morrison.'

'Why don't ye call me Jake? It's far more neighbourly.'

'Sure thing, Jake,' replied the rancher. 'And you can call me Joe.'

'Why don't you men get off'n your horses and come inside,' called Mrs Morrison. 'Coffee'll only take a minute.'

The cowboys looked inquiringly at their boss, who shrugged and began to get down from his horse. His men did the same, and soon both sides were drinking coffee and chatting away like old friends. No doubt the presence of Morrison's two pretty daughters had something to do with the younger cowboys' enthusiasm for showing their friendlier side.

Hunter was almost forgotten. Smiling

wryly to himself he slipped out of the house, mounted his horse and slowly rode away.

I never thought it was going to be *that* easy to reconcile the ranchers and the nesters! he thought contentedly as he splashed through the ford and turned his horse's head in the direction of the distant town. But then I guess it's not just my work, but His too.

SEVEN

The next day was Sunday. The preacher woke up bright and early and put on his best Sunday-go-to-Meeting suit. After making a hearty breakfast at Ma Considine's diner he went down the street to the barn that he had bought for ten dollars on his arrival in town a few days before. Now it was as clean and tidy as he could make it. It only needed chairs to be fit for worship.

When they saw the preacher go down the street Curly Watts and some of his customers picked up a couple of chairs each and carried them down to the barn. John Chapman had already loaned Hunter an old clerk's high desk from the store to take the place of a lectern.

As it got nearer to ten o'clock a steady stream of people passed down the street on their way to church. Soon the building was packed. There were just enough chairs for the womenfolk, but the children and the men had to stand. Everyone was there, Protestant, Catholic and those of no religion whatsoever.

It was a long time since the inhabitants of Antelope Wells had last seen and heard a preacher. And Hunter was no ordinary preacher. Naturally enough they were all eager to hear him preach. Some of the blither spirits had even been making bets about what he would take as his text.

A few minutes before the service was due to start the people in the church heard the sound of horses' hooves outside the building mingling with the rumbling of many wagon wheels and the jingling of harness bells as Jake Morrison's wagon rolled into town and stopped outside Hunter's impromptu church. He was followed by half a dozen other wagons.

Hunter met Morrison at the door and shook his hand warmly. 'Glad you could make it,' he said, then, noticing that although Morrison's wife and three youngest children were with him, his eldest son was not, added, 'Where's Eli?'

'Watchin' the house. To be on the safe side, like.'

Hunter smiled, 'That makes sense. The smaller ranchers may be resigned to your presence now, but I guess Bricklin isn't.'

'I tol' Eli to fire a couple of shots if he sees anyone he doesn't like the look of,' Morrison went on. 'We'll hear 'em and be back to help as quick as ever we can.'

'He seems a canny lad,' Hunter said quietly, recognizing that Morrison was more worried about leaving his son alone than he wanted to appear. 'He'll be all right.'

He smiled at the other nesters, who had descended from their wagons and had gathered in a body some way away, nervously wondering whether they were *really* welcome in town.

'Come inside, all of you. Service is just about to begin.'

As the nesters filed into the converted barn some of the townspeople eyed them askance. The nesters had made an effort to dress for the occasion, but they still looked what they were – hard-working but ill-educated farmers. They formed a tight group at the back of the barn.

Hunter began the service by welcoming everyone to his makeshift church. Then he asked the Lord to send peace to the valley and went on to say that if that was impossible they would be more than grateful if he would defend them from their enemies. It was prayer in which they all could share, and a chorus of *Amens* rose from townspeople and nesters alike.

Then he announced the first hymn, one of the old Moody and Sankey favourites. There were no hymnbooks and no music to be had in Antelope Wells, but that didn't matter too much as everyone knew both the words and the tune by heart. Hunter's rolling baritone led the singing. Townspeople and nesters joined as one to belt out the hymn until the rafters rang with sound.

Hunter had chosen to preach on a text from the fourth chapter of the book of Nehemiah. The prophet and his followers were rebuilding Jerusalem after it had been destroyed by the Babylonians. Each man was working sword in hand for fear of an attack by their enemies. One group of men was out of sight of the others, so Nehemiah told them to blow a trumpet if they were attacked and their friends would immediately come to their aid. He thought this story would strike a chord with townsmen and nesters alike.

Watching the faces of the audience as he expounded the need for them all to stand together like Nehemiah and his followers, the preacher could see that the message had struck home. The townspeople had already learned that united they could see off Deke Bricklin and his hired gunmen. Hunter's sermon was meant to show them that they had to stand shoulder to shoulder with the nesters too.

Hunter announced another hymn and once again the building filled with sound. Whatever their religious convictions, or lack of them, Western men and women loved to sing, and the opportunities for singing in small communities such as Antelope Wells were all too few.

When the service ended Hunter walked down the centre isle and took his stand by the door, ready to shake hands with the departing worshippers and speed them on their way.

The townspeople and the nesters eyed each other cautiously. Each side was afraid that a friendly advance would only be rebuffed. Then John Chapman decided that if no one else was going to start the ball rolling, he would. After all, as owner of the town's only general store he had the most to gain by opening friendly relations with the farmers. He took his wife firmly by the arm and went over to where Morrison and his family were standing. He put out his hand.

'Hallo. Welcome to Antelope Wells,' he said breezily. 'The name's Chapman. This is my wife Mary.'

'Pleased to meet you, Mr Chapman,' replied Jake Morrison, grasping the proffered hand in his work-gnarled but painfully clean fist and shaking it firmly. 'Jake Morrison's my monicker. This here's my wife Ann, and my childer Ruth, Rebecca and Zachary.' He brought another farmer forward with a sweep of his arm. 'This here's Abner Greystock, my next neighbour...'

John Chapman took the man's hand, then introduced him to the nearest townspeople, who happened to be Obadiah Somers the blacksmith and Mrs Rossiter the schoolmarm. And so the ice was broken, and the townspeople and farmers began to mingle under the approving eye of the watching Aaron Hunter.

After a while people began to want their dinners. First one couple, then a second broke away from the chatting groups and made their way towards the door.

Hunter accepted their compliments on his sermon, shook them by the hand, then opened the door. A gun blasted in the street and a bullet struck splinters from the wood beside his ear. He quickly ducked back inside the building and slammed the door.

Suddenly the makeshift church was full of

voices: women screaming with shock, men trying to calm them or worriedly asking each other a set of damnfool questions to which none of them knew the answers.

Hunter peered cautiously through a window, and was aghast to see the dusty, unshaven figure of Herb Bricklin standing in the middle of the street holding a spanking new Winchester 73. A pistol was shoved into the waistband of his pants. Someone had released him from his fetters!

A second man was standing in the shade of the disused corn-chandler's store two doors down. Two cartridge belts were slung across his chest, Mexican style. He was lazily rolling a toothpick from one side of his mouth to the other.

Hunter recognized this man. He was a gun for hire from Sonora called the Bustamente Kid. A third man was leaning on the hitching rail across the street. Hunter knew him only as Shorty. He always ran with the Bustamente Kid. There was a five-gallon can of lamp oil by his feet.

'Come and get it, preacher man,' Herb Bricklin called mockingly. 'But the rest of you townies better stay where you are if'n you don't want to get shot!'

Townsmen and nesters alike were shocked

and horrified by this turn of events. None of them was armed. The townsmen had left their weapons at home. The farmers had left theirs in their wagons.

Then the townsmen remembered the funeral, and the speed with which Hunter had drawn a hidden pistol from beneath his coat. Their eyes turned expectantly towards their marshal. He'd settle their hash. Hadn't he already sent two of Bricklin's gunmen to their graves in Boot Hill? Hadn't he outshot Herb Bricklin once already?

'You can't hide in there for ever, Marshal,' the rancher's only son called contemptuously. He knew that the preacher wasn't wearing a gun. The Kid's scruffy sidekick had found the marshal's guns, including his hideout gun, lying on his bed at the hotel. This had given the cowardly Herb Bricklin the courage to brace the marshal.

Hunter raised his eyes to heaven in silent prayer, then turned and strode up the aisle to his makeshift lectern. The worried people of Antelope Valley parted before him like the Red Sea before Moses.

He had left his prayer book unopened on the lectern throughout the service. Now he picked up the heavy brass-bound book and tucked it under his arm, then turned and made his way back to the door.

But before he could open it Theodore Dardick the gunsmith put a hand on his sleeve. 'You mustn't go out there, Marshal,' he protested. 'Not without a gun. It'd be suicide!'

There was a chorus of agreement from his congregation. In the face of this threat the differences between townspeople and farmers had completely vanished.

The preacher raised his eyebrows. 'What do you suggest I do then?' he inquired levelly.

'Keep them talking while we break down the wall at the back,' Obadiah Somers declared roundly, flexing his muscles. 'Come on, you men. It won't take us long to break out of here.'

He led a rush towards the back of the building and shoulder-charged the plank wall, which groaned in protest, but held firm. Other men began to kick at the planks with their heavy boots and pound them with their fists.

Herb Bricklin heard the sounds of crashing and banging and grinned nastily. Trying to escape, were they? He'd already thought of that and taken his precautions.

'Hey, preacher man,' he called again. 'Stop

what yer doing or I'll fire the building. Shorty here has gone and soaked the walls with lamp oil, so it'll go up like a torch. You was singing so loud ye wouldn't have noticed if he'd stolen the whole damn roof.'

It was a hot day. All the windows were open and his voice carried clearly to everyone inside the building. Somers and his team immediately stopped work on their breakout attempt.

The women began to panic. Some of them started to cry. Their menfolk tried to re-assure them but without much success. They couldn't prevent the signs of concern from showing on their own faces.

What would Hunter do, they all wondered nervously. If he went out there without a gun he was a dead man.

Peering through the windows they could see a dark trail running across the sandy street from their prison to the second gunman's feet.

Shorty fumbled in the pocket of his red-and-white chequered shirt and took out a match. He bent down and struck it on the sole of his boot, then held it up for them all to see. The gunman allowed the match to burn down almost until it reached his fingers, then blew it out.

'Come out, damn you, Marshal,' yelled Herb Bricklin. 'This is your last chance! Come out or ye'll all burn to ashes!'

He nodded to Shorty. The gunman took a second match from his pocket and lit it.

Hunter straightened his shoulders, took a firm grip on his heavy prayer book and reached for the doorhandle. A sigh of mingled relief and shame ran through the crowd. They were going to be safe after all. But was it right that one man should die for the people?

Rio Harkness was a good cowhand when he was sober. However he was rarely in that condition. He spent most of his time cadging drinks in Curly Watt's saloon. He couldn't remember the last time he'd been inside a house of religion. He'd only come this time out of sheer curiosity. But he was damned if he'd allow Hunter to go out to die without making some attempt to save him.

'Come on, you people,' he said strongly. 'Let's all go out together. They can't shoot us all.' He turned to Hunter. 'Get in the middle, preacher. You'll be OK then.'

'I'm mighty grateful for the offer, Rio,' Hunter said appreciatively. 'But it's too risky. Someone might get hurt. It's me he

131

wants. I'll go out alone.'

Clapping his hat on his head and taking the heavy prayer book in his hands he pushed open the door and went outside.

A big smile spread across Herb Bricklin's unshaven face as he saw the preacher leave the building and start to walk towards him, prayer book in hand. 'You're a lucky man, Preacher,' he said derisively. 'It's Sunday. A good day to die. You'll go straight to Heaven.'

As he spoke the Bustamente Kid spat out his toothpick and stepped down on to the sand. Across the street Shorty tossed the unused match to the ground and straightened up, his hand hovering near his gun.

The two gunmen were feeling pleased with themselves. They had ridden into town to find it all but deserted. Herb Bricklin had hailed them, given them fifty dollars to break him free from his chains and promised them another fifty if they'd help him kill the marshal.

Their horses were groundhitched nearby. All they had to do was put a couple of shots in the right place then get on to their horses and ride away. It would be the easiest hundred dollars they'd ever made.

The black-clad preacher kept on walking.

He was less than twenty yards away now. The Bustamente Kid wondered what the man thought he was doing, walking calmly into the muzzle of his employer's gun.

Herb Bricklin's angry gaze locked with his opponent's. The preacher's eyes were as hard and cold as a steel blade, and just as threatening. There was no fear in this man at all, just a boundless confidence.

Bricklin could see his death in those cold grey eyes. He levelled his Winchester and started blasting as fast as he could work the lever.

As the young rancher made his move Hunter threw himself to one side. He was only just fast enough. Bricklin's first bullet screamed past his ear and the second tore a hole in his flying coat-tails. The Bustamente Kid's first shot was a clean miss.

Like his saddle-partner, Shorty had been caught by surprise by their employer's sudden action. He hurriedly reached for his gun and triggered shot after shot at the diving preacher. The bullets spit sand in the rolling marshal's face, but made no hits.

As the preacher dived to the ground he flipped open the bulky leather-bound prayer book which had been resting on the make-shift lectern throughout the service but which he had never opened.

He didn't need to. He knew both the Holy Bible and the prayer book by heart. This book was made for another purpose. The interior had been hollowed out and contained a short-barrelled Webley Bulldog pistol. It was the twin to the one he sometimes carried in a shoulder-holster under his coat.

He had left that rig in his hotel room, thinking that if there was one place he could go to unarmed, it was a church service. But he'd been wrong.

The gun hidden in the prayer book was his last line of defence. He'd often talked about reading to badmen from the Book. Now he was going to do it in reality.

The Bustamente Kid's second bullet flew over the head of the diving Hunter. Herb Bricklin's third and fourth bullets also went wide.

Hunter's fingers closed round the butt of his pistol. The English-made weapon was double action. That meant that unlike most American-made pistols it did not need to be cocked before it could be fired. Pressure on the trigger cocked and fired it all in one motion. This made it an ideal hold-out gun.

Before his three opponents could correct

their aim the preacher rolled on to his back and triggered a shot at Herb Bricklin, then shifted his aim and pumped three bullets into the Bustamente Kid's prominent belly just above his silver embossed gunbelt. He screamed like a woman and sagged at the knees, his nickel-plated Smith & Wesson Russian pistol falling from his suddenly nerveless hand.

Ignoring the dying Bustamente Kid and the wounded Herb Bricklin the preacher came up on his elbows, levelled his gun at Shorty and squeezed the trigger. A split second later a hole appeared just above the man's fleshy nose and the back of his head blew out in a shower of blood, brains and splinters of bone that painted the wall of the harnessmaker's shop with red slime.

Hunter span round to face his remaining enemy. But Herb Bricklin had come to the end of his rope. The preacher's snap-shot had been better than he knew. The soft-nosed lead bullet had ripped through the young rancher's muscular neck, tearing the arteries wide open. Herb Bricklin was still on his feet, but the blood was pumping from his torn throat in a steady stream to dye the sand at his feet bright red.

Hunter watched with pity in his eyes as the

Winchester dropped from the young man's suddenly strengthless hands and he folded at the knees and went down. Bricklin's legs kicked once, and he was dead.

The preacher slowly got to his feet. As always after a killing he felt the weight of the dead men's sins fall heavy on his shoulders. He murmured a silent prayer for their souls. Then he bent to pick up his hat, clapped it on his head, recovered his prayer book from its resting-place on the sand near the dead Kid's right boot and tucked the Bulldog into its socket.

He was making a desultory effort to brush the sand of the road from his best suit when the first of the townspeople reached him. They were loud in their praise for his courage in going out to face the three men and his skill in disposing of them so efficiently.

The preacher shrugged them off. 'Fit them up with coffins,' he said dourly to the whiskery Jim Bacher. 'I'll bury them this afternoon. Next to the others.'

Ignoring the well-meant efforts of the townspeople to get him to come with them to the saloon for a celebratory drink, he strode away in the direction of the hotel. Right now he needed to be alone.

Behind him the crowd slowly dispersed. The farmers hitched up their wagons and set off on the long drive home. Mothers dragged their children away from the bloody ground and went home to get dinner ready for their men. The men went into the saloon.

Curly Watts hummed to himself as he served up the drinks. He'd sure be sorry when the preacher finally left Antelope Wells. Life with him around was both entertaining and pretty damn profitable.

EIGHT

That afternoon Hunter buried Herb Bricklin's two hired guns. After all, they had no relatives to care where they were buried. But Herb Bricklin's father was living only a few miles away. He had the right to bury his own son.

Like the rest of the townspeople, Jim Bacher thought Hunter was crazy to take the young man's body back to the D-B Connected. 'Bricklin'll kill you sure,' said the whiskery old carpenter as he coffined up the body and helped the preacher load it onto a borrowed buckboard.

John Chapman was even more blunt. 'You're mad! Quite mad,' he said shaking his head in disbelief.

The preacher smiled sadly. 'I know it's risky, but I have to do it. It's only right Bricklin should have the opportunity to bury his own son.'

Mrs Considine threw up her hands in despair. 'You'll be killed, and then where will we be? Deke Bricklin will ride right over us. And what will happen to my Mary then?'

There was a general murmur of agreement from the assembled townspeople. The preacher had given them hope. With him to lead them they had stood off Bricklin once already. But no one could take his place if he were killed, as seemed all too likely.

Only wise old Doc Thompson disagreed. 'Let the man do what he thinks is best,' he urged them. 'He hasn't been wrong yet, has he?'

It was true and they all knew it. The townspeople's protests subsided into faint mutterings.

Theodore Dardick the gunsmith wrapped it all up neatly for them. 'Whatever we say, Mr Hunter will do just what he wants to. We must hope it all turns out for the best. Maybe he can make Deke Bricklin see that if he doesn't make peace with us there'll be more deaths.'

He turned to face the blandly smiling preacher. 'But I'd be much happier if you'd take one of my shotguns with you, marshal. There's nothing like a shotgun to make folks think twice about pulling a gun on a feller.'

Hunter grinned. 'That's true enough. I accept with pleasure.'

So when the preacher finally drove his

borrowed buckboard out of town with Herb Bricklin's coffin bouncing around under a tarp in the back he had one pistol under his coat, another in the holster belted round his waist, a Winchester under his feet and a sawn-off shotgun on the seat beside him.

A crowd of townspeople had gathered to see him off. A number of the women were weeping quietly into their handkerchiefs. They didn't expect to see him come back alive.

The trail leading from town to the Bricklin ranch ran beside the river for the first mile or so then curved gently away from the slowly moving stream and on to a bench that ran parallel to the water about a hundred yards away. Drifting sand was already beginning to fill the ruts in the trail. Few people went that way since Bricklin had switched his business from Antelope Wells to Mariposa, over the hills to the north.

Hunter kept up a fast pace. He wanted to deliver the body to the ranch and return to town before nightfall.

He was barely a couple of miles out of town when he saw two men sitting in the shade of a big cottonwood tree down by the river. They were enjoying a companionable smoke. Their horses were grazing peacefully alongside them.

When they saw the preacher coming their way they tossed their smokes aside, clambered on to their horses' backs and came racing towards him.

Hunter ignored them at first, but when one of the men whipped his rifle to his shoulder and sent a bullet whistling over his head he hauled on the reins and brought the buckboard to a halt.

He reached under the seat for the sawn-off shotgun that Dardick the gunsmith had given him. It was the best weapon for use at close quarters.

Moments later the two gunmen drew alongside the buckboard. One of them was young, slim as a snake, and to Hunter's experienced eyes, just as deadly. He wore two guns in Slim-Jim fast-draw holsters and had a brand new Winchester 73 carbine in his hands.

His companion was older, fatter and more slovenly in his dress, though his Colt Model 1860.44 pistol looked well cared for. When he looked at Hunter his eyes were like stones, empty of all human feeling.

The younger man might kill for pay or for pleasure, Hunter thought disgustedly, but this man would kill you with no more emotion than he'd feel when stepping on a bug.

The preacher swung up the sawn-off shotgun so that it was pointing between the two men, held back the hammers with his thumb and squeezed both the triggers. The double click was loud enough to make the two gunmen's horses' ears twitch nervously. Now if anything happened to loosen Hunter's grip on the shotgun the hammers would fall, the shotgun would fire and their guts would be splattered all over the landscape.

The two men exchanged nervous glances. Hunter had neatly neutralized their advantage in firepower.

'Holster your guns,' Hunter snapped, emphasizing his words with a slight movement of his shotgun. The older man scowled blackly, but holstered his Colt. The younger man hesitated a moment longer, then slipped his Winchester back into its boot with a faint shrug. Both men kept their hands well away from their guns.

'Hey, aren't you the new marshal of Antelope Wells?' the younger man said with an attempt at bravado. 'What the hell are you doin' out here? Way off your home range, ain't you?'

Hunter kept his voice level. 'I'm on my way to visit with your boss. I've got something for him.'

The young gunny raised his eyebrows. 'What's that then?'

'You can look if you like,' Hunter said dryly. 'But keep your hands away from your guns. Any funny business and your friend here gets a load of buckshot right where it'll do most good.'

Nodding his acceptance of this arrangement the young gunny twitched his reins and his horse sidled delicately down the side of the buckboard.

The other man kept his hands clasped over his saddle horn. A muscle twitched in his unshaven cheek. The twin barrels of the shotgun were aimed right at his brisket. At this range the double load of buckshot would blow a hole in him the size of a dinner plate.

The young gunny leaned over and twitched the tarp aside. 'What have you got in the box?' he inquired curiously.

Hunter shrugged. 'Why not take a look?'

The gunny swung down out of the saddle and climbed into the back of the buckboard. He heaved at the lid of the long wooden box. It had only been lightly nailed down, and the nails soon gave way with a screech of tortured wood. The gunny flipped the lid aside and peered into the box, then recoiled with a vivid oath.

'It's the boss's son,' he gasped. 'He's been shot.'

For a moment a faint smile appeared on his companion's impassive countenance, then it was gone. He'd never cottoned to Herb Bricklin anyway.

The young gunman replaced the lid and pulled the tarp over it again. 'Who shot him, marshal?' he asked. 'You?'

'That's right,' replied Hunter evenly.

The young gunny stared at the black-clad preacher in amazement. 'And you're bringing the old man the body?' He shook his head wonderingly. 'Hell, man! You must be as crazy as a bed-bug. He'll kill you fer sure.'

'I hope not. I aim to make him see that his vendetta against Antelope Wells has got to stop,' Hunter explained. 'It's already killed five men. Including his son...'

'Five, you say?' the gunman repeated incredulously.

'That's right. Two on Thursday, and three today.'

'I already know you killed Kit Berry and Bunco Green,' the young gunny replied sourly. 'As fer the other three, I can see one of 'em, right there. Who were the others?'

'The Bustamente Kid and a fella that rode with him called Shorty,' Hunter declared. 'They came riding into Antelope Wells while I was in church. Your boss's son hired them to free him and then kill me.' His mouth twitched briefly. 'I buried the two of them this afternoon. I thought your boss would rather bury his son himself.'

The two gunmen regarded Hunter with new respect. They had heard of the Bustamente Kid. He was a real badman, fast with a gun and none too scrupulous about who he used it on. This man sitting so quiet under their questions must be hell on wheels with a gun.

But that didn't make him any the less of a fool, did it? Didn't he realize that he was asking for trouble, bringing Bricklin the body of his son? More than likely there would be two buryings out at the D-B Connected, not one.

The young gunman remounted his horse. 'You wanted to go to the boss's ranch,' he grinned. 'Then get to it. I ain't about ter try and stop you.'

'Well, thank you for that,' replied Hunter sardonically.

'What's more, I'll ride in with you, just to make sure you don't get shot up by the other sentries,' the gunman added with a grin. 'I sure don't want to miss being there when you tell the boss how you shot his son!'

He turned to his companion. 'You stay here, Patterson. I'll send someone out to join you when I get back to the ranch.'

Hunter promptly switched his aim from the man Patterson to the one who was doing all the talking. Patterson breathed a hearty sigh of relief, then urged his horse into a trot and rode away in the direction of the river.

'Lead on,' said Hunter, gathering the reins in one hand and keeping the shotgun trained on the young gunman with the other. He flicked the reins and the buckboard lurched into motion.

When Hunter and his escort turned in through the ranch gates a number of hard-eyed gunnies were lazing on the stoop. They watched with interest as Hunter brought the buckboard to a halt in front of the ranch house.

'Afternoon, boys,' the young gunman said gaily. 'Look what I found on the trail. It's the new marshal of Antelope Wells.'

That woke them up a mite. So this was the man who'd shot Berry and Green! Some of these men had been friends of the two dead men. They cursed and swore at Hunter for a murderer and called loudly for a rope.

Hunter made a warning gesture with the sawn-off shotgun and the angry cries subsided, but he knew that the situation was on a knife edge.

The sound of angry voices brought Ben Strutt out of the house. He saw Hunter and touched his hat in an ironical gesture. 'How d'ye do, marshal. Welcome to the D-B Connected.'

'Good afternoon, Mr Strutt,' the preacher replied with equal politeness. 'If it's possible, I should like to speak to Mr Bricklin.'

'Go fetch the boss,' Ben Strutt ordered one of the nearby men sharply. He nodded in the direction of the shotgun, which was now pointing right at his brisket. 'Ain't your thumbs getting a mite tired o' holdin' those hammers, marshal? Why not put that thing down and give yerself a rest?'

Hunter treated this suggestion with the contempt it deserved. If he once relaxed his grip on the shotgun these men would shoot him to doll rags.

Deke Bricklin stumped out of the house. He glared at Hunter, totally ignoring the yawning muzzles of the shotgun that the preacher had immediately pointed his way. He was still sore from the beating he'd been given. He wouldn't forget *that* in a hurry.

'You've got a hell of a nerve, coming here!' spat the burly rancher. 'What do you want, anyway? Speak your piece and get out.'

'I've got bad news for you,' Hunter said evenly. 'Your son...'

Bricklin's jaw clenched. 'What about my son?' he demanded angrily.

'He's dead!'

The big man seemed to sag. 'How?'

'He and two other men tried to shoot it out with me earlier today. They lost. I've brought you his body.'

Deke Bricklin jumped down off the stoop and hurried across the sandy yard to where the buckboard was standing. He removed the tarp, then levered aside the lid of the rough coffin. For a moment or two he stood gazing at the bloody body of his son.

This was the end of all his dreams. He had built up his ranch as an inheritance for the boy. He had no other living relatives. Now that his son was dead there was no point in going on. He drew his nickel-plated Merwin

& Hulbert revolver and put the muzzle between his lips. His finger tightened on the trigger.

'Stop!' commanded Hunter in a voice of iron. 'Suicide is a sin. Do you want to go to Hell?'

Dazed, Deke Bricklin took the muzzle of the pistol out of his mouth and looked at it wonderingly. Had he really been about to blow his brains all over the landscape?

'Thanks, mister,' he said shakily. 'I don't know what I was doin' there for a moment.'

'It was the shock of seeing your son's body,' the preacher said sympathetically.

The rancher turned his head and called, 'Bill, Neuces! Take Herb's body into the house.'

The two gunmen did as they were told.

When Bricklin turned back to face the preacher his expression was bitter and cold. He opened his mouth...

Hunter got in first. 'Maybe *now* you'll change your evil ways, Deke Bricklin!' he said warningly. 'You've been acting the tyrant in this valley for far too long, bullying the townspeople, threatening the farmers, killing people who opposed you. Thought there was no one to stop you, eh?

'Old Pharaoh thought the same as you. He

tried to oppress the Children of Israel, and guess what happened? God took his son. Now he has taken yours too.'

Deep in the rancher's little piggy eyes a glint of red showed for a moment and was gone. He longed to give his men the word to blast the interfering, sanctimonious stranger off the seat of his buckboard. But he had too much sense for that. One wrong move and he'd get a bellyful of buckshot balls, and he knew he'd find them mighty indigestible. Deke Bricklin stared at Hunter with hate in his eyes.

'I owe you something for bringing my son's body back to me, marshal,' he grated. 'But don't push it. Maybe you'd get me with that scatter-gun, and maybe you wouldn't. But I could have you killed just by snapping my fingers.'

It was true enough. Bricklin's men were just itching to draw their guns and cut down on the man who had shot their bunkies. Their attention was fixed on the black-clad figure of the preacher and their hands were hovering near their guns.

'I won't do it, though,' Bricklin added grimly. 'It's not worth the risk. I'll kill you another time, and you can damn well bank on that, Mister Preacher-man! I'm declaring open season on you and everyone else in this valley.'

There was a murmur of astonishment and anticipatory pleasure from his band of gunmen. Until now they had been kept on a tight rein. Were the gloves coming off at last? God, how they hoped so!

'This valley was going to be my kingdom,' Bricklin said bitterly, 'and my son's after me. That's all gone now, thanks to you. All I've got left is revenge. You can tell the folks in Antelope Wells that if they don't move out I'll burn 'em out, and that goes for the nesters too.'

Flecks of foam had appeared at the corners of his mouth. Hunter thought the shock of his son's death had probably turned his brain.

'Now get out of here, marshal! Next time I see you I'll kill you!'

Totally ignoring the threat of Hunter's shotgun the grief-stricken rancher turned and strode heavily back into the house.

Taking a swift glance round the yard, Hunter realized that Deke Bricklin's gunmen were as shocked by his behaviour as the preacher was himself. But that wouldn't last for long. He whipped up the horses and rattled out of the ranchyard before they came to their senses and realized that they would never have a better chance to kill him.

Once he was out of the ranchyard he released the tension on the hammers of his shotgun. Dardick had been right. There was something about a shotgun that made men walk mighty carefully.

It was no use out here on the plain, though. Its effective range was much too short. He stuffed the gun down under the seat and took out his Winchester and rested it across his knees.

The preacher urged the horses along, snatching quick glances over his shoulder every now and then. He had gone more than half-way back to town when he saw a plume of dust rising into the air behind him and realized that he was being pursued.

Maybe Deke Bricklin had come to his senses and ordered his men to try and kill him, or maybe Ben Strutt had taken it upon himself to give the order. Not that it mattered that much.

Hunter didn't like using the whip, but sometimes it was necessary. He drew it from its socket and cracked it along his horses' flanks. They increased their pace to a gallop.

He had got a good start, two good horses

and the buckboard was empty, so the preacher wasn't too worried that the band of gunmen would catch him before he reached the safety of the town.

He had forgotten about Patterson. The taciturn gunman had ambled back to his place in the cottonwoods fringing the river and built himself a smoke while he waited for his companion or a replacement to rejoin him. When he saw the racing buckboard coming his way, followed at full pelt by a band of riders, he climbed into the saddle and started riding towards the road, choosing a course that would intercept Hunter about a mile from the town.

Hunter whipped up his horses until the blood-flecked foam streamed away from their straining mouths, but soon realized that he would have to deal with Patterson himself if he wanted to reach the town alive.

Soon Patterson's racing horse brought him to within a couple of hundred yards of the trail. The gunman drew his Henry repeater from its boot and began to lever shot after shot at the speeding buckboard.

Hunter realized with disgust that the man wasn't trying to hit him at all. It was his horses the gunman was aiming at. In a way it made sense. The horses were a much bigger target, and if one of them took a bullet and went down the buckboard would probably roll over and throw him out. If he weren't killed on the spot he'd be so badly injured that Bricklin's men would be able to finish him off at their leisure.

Wrapping the reins round his left wrist, Hunter took up his Winchester 73 and took a shot at the charging Patterson, but the buckboard was living up to its name and his bullets went wide.

Then the gunman reached the trail and swung in behind the speeding buckboard. The preacher couldn't fire back without turning completely round on his seat. If he did that he'd likely lose control of the vehicle.

Slowly but surely Patterson was catching up on the speeding buckboard. Hunter's back crawled as shot after shot whistled past his ears. He hunkered down on the seat as best he could. It would be a close-run thing whether he would get into Antelope Wells before Patterson put a bullet into his back.

The town was closer now. Surely the townspeople would hear the shots and come out into the street to see what was going on? If Patterson saw people gathering on the street with guns he might sheer off and let the speeding buckboard escape to safety.

The preacher turned his head and snatched a quick glance behind him. Patterson was less than fifty yards behind him now and was lashing his horse into even greater efforts. It was only the difficulty of shooting from a galloping horse that had kept Hunter alive for so long.

Suddenly a puff of smoke bloomed from a window of one of the buildings at the edge of town, which was now less than three hundred yards away. A split second later Hunter heard a bullet whip past his head.

A moment later Jim Bacher stepped out into the street. The whiskery old carpenter was holding his ancient Hawken rifle and capering with joy.

Hunter risked a quick backward glance. A body was lying in the dust of the trail a hundred yards behind him. Beside it, nuzzling his master's body in sad puzzlement, was the man's palomino gelding. The old-timer had shot Patterson off his horse. By doing so he had probably saved the preacher's life.

Hunter heaved a sigh of relief and hauled on the reins. The racing buckboard began to slow down. But he was going too fast to stop just yet. As he shot past Bacher he waved his hat and yelled his thanks, eventually managing to pull the sweating and foam-flecked horses to a stop outside the saloon.

By now the streets were full of men with guns. Bricklin's riders saw this and reined in their horses well out of rifle range. They huddled together for a moment in talk, then one man rode cautiously forward and came to a halt beside Patterson's body.

The gunman got down off his horse, heaved Patterson across the palomino's saddle, and led horse and man back to join the others. Then the band of gunmen wheeled their horses and rode back to the D-B Connected.

NINE

The preacher posted two sentries, one at each end of the town, then called all the remaining citizens of Antelope Wells to a meeting in the saloon and gave them Bricklin's message.

The citizens were solidly behind the idea of making a stand. They had had enough of Bricklin and his gunnies throwing their weight about. That was why they had chosen Bill Lonegan for mayor.

Maybe that hadn't worked out too well for Lonegan, but they'd got the preacher to help them now, and his confidence in their ability to defeat Deke Bricklin and his men if they all stood shoulder to shoulder had put steel into their backbones. The preacher's successes with a gun had encouraged them too.

'The score so far is Christians five, Lions nil!' Doc Thompson remarked cheerfully.

'Six, Doc, six!' Jim Bacher protested vehemently. 'Don't fergit the varmint I got!'

There was a roar of laughter from the other men in the saloon. The preacher held up a hand and the noise died away.

'It was a very good shot, Jim,' he said approvingly. 'Let's hope you'll be as accurate next time.'

'Ye can rely on me, marshal,' Bacher declared proudly, and took a swig at his whiskey. 'Ol' Betsy is a straight-shootin' gun, and that ain't no lie!'

'Who else is a good shot with a rifle?' asked Hunter.

Harry Rose, Theo Dardick, a couple of the saloon loafers whose names Hunter didn't yet know, Steve Harbin the saddler and the clerk from the hotel, a young German immigrant named Bauer, put up their hands.

'Right! If we're attacked I want Rosey on the roof of the blacksmith's shop. You stay where you are, Jim. Your place has got a good field of fire.'

'I guess I already proved that,' Bacher confirmed, cackling into his beer.

'I want you two men in the buildings at the far end of the street,' Hunter told the saloon loafers. 'The hotel roof would make a good firing position for you, Theo. The rest of you can choose your own spots.

'Chapman, if they break through the barriers, run upstairs and get ready to shoot into the street from a top-floor window. The same applies to you, Bauer.'

'*Ja*! I tink so,' agreed the young German with a nod of the head. 'I shoot goot. You see.'

The preacher's grey eyes moved from face to face. They all looked serious, but determined.

'Tomorrow I'm going to post lookouts on both sides of town, so if they come we'll have plenty of warning. That means you can go about your business as normal, but for God's sake keep your guns handy. I imagine Bricklin will try to get it done quickly, if he can.'

Rio Harkness shifted his quid into his cheek and spat a long stream of tobacco juice into the spittoon. 'Are ye goin' ter call fer help, marshal?' he drawled.

'No,' Hunter replied. 'The governor's already sent all the help he can spare.' A thin smile flickered across his face. 'Me!'

There was a brief silence before he went on: 'Anyway, with God's help the folks of Antelope Wells will deal with Deke Bricklin by their ownselves. Isn't that right?'

There was a roar of agreement from the crowd of men. The preacher said no more, and the townsmen, realizing that he had finished making his arrangements, bellied up to the bar and roared to Curly Watts to refill their glasses. As the drinks went down the boasting grew so loud that if Deke Bricklin and his men could have heard them they might have decided it was best to ride out of the valley with their tails between their legs.

Or maybe not. They were talking big tonight, the preacher thought sardonically, but how many of them will stand up and be counted tomorrow when hot lead begins to fly?

The following morning the preacher left John Chapman in charge and rode out of town. He didn't like leaving Antelope Wells at such a critical juncture, but he had no choice. He wanted to warn the nesters that Deke Bricklin had sworn to burn them out and invite them to move into town until the trouble was over.

It won't be easy to get those sodbusters to abandon their homes, he thought dourly, as he reined in his horse on the near side of the ford and raked the land on the far side with his field-glasses.

The six sod huts looked built to last. Smoke was rising from their chimneys as the womenfolk cooked up their men's midday meal. The preacher could see children playing in the dooryards and men working in the fields. It was a peaceful scene, and Hunter felt sad at having to spoil it.

Jake Morrison was busy ploughing when the preacher rode across the ford and on to his land. The farmer saw who was coming and waved, but kept the plough moving across the field to the far side, then turned his team and came back towards Hunter. The freshly turned earth was a rich brown colour and looked mighty fertile.

The preacher sat his horse and watched the moving plough and its straining horses with a mixture of approval and regret. He knew that the future of this part of the West *was* in farming, not ranching. But he was a cattleman at heart, not a farmer. Deep down he hated to see the grassland vanish under the plough. Right now he could sympathize with Bricklin and the other ranchers.

When Morrison reached the side of the field where Hunter was waiting he halted the team, took off his hat and wiped his forehead with a red bandanna.

'Mornin' marshal,' he said breezily. 'What brings you out here on this fine summer's mornin'?'

'Bad news, I'm afraid,' the preacher replied soberly. 'Deke Bricklin has sworn to burn you all out. The town too. I want you and your friends to pack up and move into town until this business is over.'

Morrison's jaw clenched. 'We ain't movin',' he said aggressively. 'We can defend ourselves. You saw that fer yerself!'

'Not against more than thirty hired killers,' Hunter replied soberly. 'Nor against fire.'

'Me 'n Eli can keep 'em off with our rifles,' Morrison objected.

'For how long?' said Hunter with a lift of the eyebrows. 'And what if you catch a bullet? What happens to your family then?'

'You won't frighten me thataway, marshal,' Morrison said sturdily. 'Ma and me had all that out before we agreed to come out West. We weighed up the risks, from Indians and such, and made up our minds to give it our best shot.' He shrugged. 'If we die, we die. But we ain't lettin' no rich rancher drive us off our land. And that's flat!'

'You might be able to hold out, Morrison,' the preacher said harshly. 'You've got plenty of guns and people to use them. But what about your neighbours? The Prynnes are

164

nearest to Bricklin's ranch. There's only the two of them. How long do you think they'll stand against twenty hired guns? Hector Mackay and his wife are the next along. They've got two small children. You won't hear their screams when Bricklin's men set fire to their little home, it's too far away, but you'll think you can. The Greystocks have four young ones, none of them big enough to hold a pistol. The Quayles and the Wrights might make a fight of it, for a while; they've got five strapping sons between them, but all Bricklin has to do is wait for the night, then sneak up and shoot into the house through the loopholes.

'As for you,' he said cynically, 'if they can't get you out any other way they'll blast you out with dynamite.'

Morrison's jaw fell open, 'Would Bricklin do that?' he gasped.

'Yes, he would,' the preacher said levelly. 'The shock of his son's death has unhinged his brain. Now all he wants is revenge. On me, on you sodbusters, and on the town. He's got the men to do it too. Some of them would kill their grandmothers for a dollar. The rest would do it for fun.'

He gestured across the peaceful fields. 'This settlement is indefensible. You can't help your friends and they can't help you. If you don't leave here right away Bricklin and his men will destroy you one by one.'

It was true, and Morrison had to accept it.

'OK,' he said reluctantly. 'I suppose you're right. What do you want me to do?'

'Help me persuade the others to come into town.'

'I guess I can do that.'

'You must bring everything with you when you come,' the preacher insisted. 'And I mean *everything*. Bricklin will burn your homes, there's nothing we can do about that, but you don't have to lose anything else.'

'But where shall we live?' Morrison asked uncertainly.

The Preacher laughed sourly. 'That's the least of your worries. There are more than enough empty houses in Antelope Wells for all of you.'

Morrison turned and took a long look at his sod hut, built with such labour and pride. Well, he could do it again if he had to. That was what being a pioneer was all about.

'OK, marshal,' he said grimly. 'If we gotta do it, then we'd better make a start.'

The Preacher sat his horse and rolled

himself a smoke while Morrison guided his plough-team back to the farm, unhitched the horse from the plough, swopped the leading reins for a riding bridle and bit and strapped an old McClellan saddle on to the beast. Then he took up his old Ballard and a belt of shells, clambered into the saddle and rode back to where Hunter was waiting.

'Right, marshal,' he said grimly. 'Let's go to the Quayles first. They're the nearest.'

The preacher returned to Antelope Wells late that afternoon, riding at the head of a convoy of wagons. Jake Morrison was driving the lead wagon. His wife was sitting by his side. The wagon was piled high with all their worldly possessions. They had left nothing behind them for Bricklin's men to burn. Their three younger children were riding on the tailboard. Eli was walking beside the wagon, leading their dairy cow.

Behind them came five more wagons. Each one was loaded with a nester family's furniture and other personal belongings. They looked as though they were about to set off on the long journey to California.

The sound of the creaking wagon wheels and rattling chains brought the citizens of Antelope Wells out of their homes and places of business to watch the farmers arrive in town.

The preacher held up his hand and the wagons rumbled to a halt. The farmers looked around them nervously, gripping their guns. They only had the marshal's word for it that they were welcome in town.

John Chapman stepped up to Morrison's wagon. He had a welcoming smile on his face.

'It's a damn shame you've had to leave your homes,' he said sympathetically, holding out his hand to the surprised farmer, 'but we'll all do our best to make you feel at home in Antelope Wells until this fuss with Bricklin is over and done with.'

There was a murmur of agreement and approval from the crowd of townspeople. Farmers weren't usually all that welcome in Western towns, but with Bricklin expected to attack any day now their guns would be a mighty useful addition to the defence. And as Hunter had pointed out, when this ruckus was over and the farmers went back to their homesteads they would need supplies and where else would they get them?

The farmers exchanged surprised glances. The citizens of Antelope Wells had never been keen to see them before.

Jake Morrison climbed down from his seat on the lead wagon and took the storekeeper's hand in his. 'We're right grateful to you people for taking us in,' he replied gruffly.

'It is the Christian thing to do,' John Chapman said virtuously, giving the impassive Hunter a sly glance from under the edge of his hatbrim. The preacher smiled blandly, but said nothing.

Then Chapman raised his voice and addressed the other farmers. 'There's a building set aside for each family. These people will show you where.'

A number of married couples had collected behind him. On his signal one couple went to each wagon and introduced themselves to the farmer and his family. They had been given the job of settling the new arrivals in their temporary homes.

The wagons slowly rolled away down the street, each one pulling up outside the house or shop that had been allocated to that particular family. As soon as each wagon reached its destination a group of townsmen arrived and started to unload it.

The preacher watched all this with some satisfaction. He had commissioned Chapman and Doc Thompson to arrange all this while he went out to persuade the farmers and their families to abandon their farms and come into town. It looked as though the two men had done a good job.

The remaining townspeople slowly dispersed, chattering to themselves animatedly. Antelope Wells had been a sleepy little town, but not any more. Not since the preacher had ridden into town and turned things upside down.

That evening all the womenfolk were invited to Mrs Rossiter's house for a sewing-bee. Of course that was just an excuse for a good gossip and get-to-know you session. The men went to the saloon.

Everyone was there. Curly Watts was almost run off his feet. His bar had never been so busy. Not that he minded. The only thing that worried Curly was whether he would run out of beer and whiskey before the fight with Bricklin had ended.

At first the farmers felt a bit out of place but the townspeople were friendly and their initial doubts soon disappeared in a wave of good fellowship.

Other alliances were also in the wind. Young Eli Morrison had been struck all of a heap by pretty Mary Considine and the Quayle and Wright boys had also noticed that there were a number of pretty girls in town.

Next day the preacher went up on to the roof of the hotel and scanned the country with his field-glasses. He was fully expecting Bricklin to make a move today. The question was: would he attack the town head-on or leave the citizens to stew while he went for the softer target provided by the nesters?

All seemed peaceful at first and he sat down and rolled himself a smoke while he waited for something to happen. Sure enough, it wasn't long before something did. A plume of dust down the valley showed that a big band of riders was coming this way.

But instead of heading for the town the riders forked off left and crossed the river at a ford lower down. They were heading straight for the little group of sod huts.

The Preacher deliberated for a second or two, then clattered down the stairs and ran down the street to the stable. His horse was saddled up and ready to go.

The tall, thin Mark Tiverton raised his eyebrows. 'What's all the hurry, marshal?'

'Bricklin has sent his men to burn the farmers' homes,' the preacher replied brusquely, swinging himself into the saddle.

'Tell Chapman I'm off to blunt them some, will you?'

'Sure thing, marshal,' the beanpole livery-man replied, grinning. He could guess what Hunter meant by 'blunt them some' and thoroughly approved. 'Give 'em hell, won't you?'

'That's exactly what I aim to do,' Hunter replied seriously. 'Men who'll burn down another man's home deserve everything they get, in this world and the next.'

Hunter rode out of town without a backward glance. The townspeople had their orders. Even if Bricklin sent a second group of men to attack the town in his absence they ought to be OK until he could get back to help them.

The plume of dust raised by the pounding hooves of Deke Bricklin's posse of gunmen was heading straight for Prynne's soddy, which was the nearest of the soddies to Bricklin's ranch.

The Preacher could see that he wouldn't be able to get there first, so he headed up the valley towards Morrison's farm. He crossed the river, spurred over the plough-land at a gallop and plunged into the broken ground at the foot of the hills through which he'd come on his first visit to the nesters.

Praying that he hadn't been seen by the oncoming band of gunmen the Preacher threaded his way through the rocks and scrubby trees that clothed the foot of the slope. Above him the red sandstone cliffs reared high into the sky. It took him the best part of an hour to get to within rifle-shot of the Prynnes' soddy.

By then the building was already in flames. Bricklin's men were riding round their handiwork, whooping with glee and firing their pistols in the air. The Preacher couldn't tell whether they realized that the soddy was empty, or just didn't care. They certainly weren't expecting to meet any opposition though.

Hunter swung down out of the saddle and looped his reins over a handy tree-branch. He took his Winchester from its boot and worked the lever to bring a shell under the hammer. Then he found a good position far enough away from his horse to be sure that when the shooting started it wouldn't be hit by a stray shot. He rested the barrel of his Winchester on the top of a flat rock, took careful aim at one of the cavorting riders and gently squeezed the trigger.

As the sound of the shot echoed off the cliffs behind him the man he'd shot at dropped his pistol and slid gently out of the saddle and fell to the ground. Before the other men could react Hunter chose another target, lined up his sights on the man's chest, and fired. The gunman jerked as the bullet hit him, then let go of the reins and slumped over his saddlebow, either badly wounded or dead. His horse, puzzled by his rider's behaviour, took a couple of steps forward and then began to graze.

The sound of the second shot made other riders scatter in panic. They hadn't been expecting anyone to fight back. Some of them dug their heels into their horses' sides and thundered out of the Prynne's dooryard, hoping to get out of range of the deadly rifle. Other men threw themselves off their horses and took cover as best they could behind rocks and trees.

The angry gunmen sent a torrent of lead towards the place from which the fatal bullets had come. But as soon as the Preacher had fired his second shot he'd abandoned his post and slipped through the undergrowth to a new position.

The Preacher took aim at a burly gunman in a chequered shirt. He centred the sights on the man's chest and squeezed the trigger, but as his gun barked the man moved slightly and the bullet hit him in the right shoulder.

'Aagh, I'm shot,' cried the gunman, slumping to the ground with his back against a tree, his left hand going to the point of his shoulder where blood was already dyeing the cloth bright red.

Hot lead lashed the bushes over Hunter's head like hail as the other gunmen fired back, but Hunter had already eeled away.

Suddenly a man broke cover and ran towards his fallen comrade. Hunter could have shot the good samaritan easily enough, but instead of squeezing the trigger he lowered his muzzle and watched the gunman drag the wounded man away.

The Preacher was pleased to see that at least one of the gunmen had some good in him. In his experience most gunmen couldn't give a damn what happened to their companions.

The good samaritan dragged his wounded companion into the shelter of a large rock, then took off his hat and waved it once over his head before ducking down out of sight.

It was his way of expressing his thanks to the unseen rifleman for his life.

Maybe he can still be saved, the Preacher thought speculatively. If we meet up again I won't shoot him unless I'm forced to.

Hunter drew a bead on a man who was trying to organize an advance on his former position. His rifle cracked and the man threw up his arms and fell backwards out of sight. The other men dove for cover. The attack had ended before it had even begun.

Hunter smiled grimly. These men weren't very good at soldiering. No doubt they were fine at bullying harmless farmers or bush-whacking careless travellers, maybe most of them would be willing to fight it out in the main street at noon with another gunman, but few men were keen on facing a will o' the wisp who shot men down from cover and only needed one bullet to settle each man.

Bricklin's men soon decided they had suffered enough. They pulled back, firing wildly as they went, leaving the bodies of their three dead companions where they lay.

Hunter let them go.

That was a good morning's work, he thought contentedly as he dragged the bodies into the shade of a big rock to await collection and later burial. He had taken out four of Bricklin's men at no cost to himself and only one of the soddies had been set alight.

By the time he had made his way back to his horse and ridden down on to the flat land by the river, the defeated gunmen were well on their way back to the ranch.

Maybe the failure of their attempt to burn all the nesters' houses will make their employer give up his desire for revenge, the Preacher thought hopefully. Maybe their losses will encourage some of Bricklin's hired guns to seek easier employment elsewhere.

He doubted it though. The Devil had got hold of Deke Bricklin now and he wasn't about to let go. As for the rancher's men, most of them had sold their souls to the Devil long ago.

Two horses were plodding along well behind the main body. The Preacher took his field-glasses from his saddle-bag and focused on them. As he had thought, it was the wounded man and his friend. The others had left them to make their way back to the ranch as best they could.

As he watched, the leading horse suddenly turned sharply to the left and headed straight for Antelope Wells. The Preacher thought he knew why. The wounded man must have been hit harder than he had thought. His friend had decided to take him into town to be tended by Doc Thompson.

But will the townsfolk let him do it? Hunter asked himself thoughtfully. Almost certainly not. They hate Bricklin's men, and with good reason. They'll probably try to shoot both men. Or hang them.

The Preacher wasn't having that. The wounded man was no danger to anyone now, and he needed help badly. His friend was both brave and loyal. Both men deserved better than to be shot down like dogs by an angry townsman or farmer.

Hunter dug his heels into his horse's side and set off on a course that would catch up with the pair of slow moving horses just before they reached the town.

TEN

The preacher caught up with the two men half a mile outside town. He wasn't expecting either man to show fight, but he drew his gun just in case.

As he rode up the unwounded gunman brought both horses to a halt and raised his hands in the air. He was a stocky man, with rusty red hair and an open, weatherbeaten face. Hunter thought he was probably pushing forty, but not too hard.

'I won't give you no trouble, marshal,' the man said hastily, eyeing the silver star on Hunter's vest with alarm. 'I was heading fer town already. Cole here needs the doc real bad.'

'So I see,' Hunter replied dryly.

The wounded man was slumped over his saddlebow. Despite the makeshift bandage round his shoulder the right-hand side of his shirt was drenched with blood.

'The doc'll be able to patch Cole up again, won't he?' the red-headed gunman said hopefully.

The preacher shrugged. 'Maybe. From the looks of things he's lost a lot of blood though.'

'Then fer God's sake let me get him to the doc before it's too late!'

'Give me your gun first. Carefully now.'

The red-haired gunman took his pistol from his holster and handed it to Hunter, holding it by the barrel. Hunter stuck it in his waistband.

'Now your rifle.'

The gunman did as he was told. 'Now can we go?' he said agitatedly. His friend was swaying in the saddle as he slipped in and out of consciousness.

'OK. Lead on,' said Hunter.

The worried gunman kicked his horse into a gentle walk afraid to go too fast in case the wounded man fell off his horse and afraid to go too slow in case his friend upped and died before he could get him to a doctor.

Hunter rode on the wounded man's other side, ready to catch him if he fell.

'What's your name, anyway?' the preacher inquired of the red-haired gunman.

'Richard Timms. But they usually call me Rusty. This here's Cole Morris.'

Their names didn't ring any bells in the preacher's mind. There were no Wanted posters out on either man as far as he knew.

'Why do *you* care what happens to this man?' the preacher said curiously. He cocked his head in the direction of the distant dustcloud that hid the retreating band of gunmen. 'Your friends didn't give a damn for him, did they?'

The red-haired gunman bridled angrily. 'They're no friends of mine,' he snapped. 'It was Cole's idea to come here. We was fresh out of cash an' Deke Bricklin was offerin' good wages. But if we'd knowed what the job was gonna be we wouldn't have come.'

The preacher raised his eyebrows. 'Are you telling me you didn't like what you were doing for Deke Bricklin?'

'I sure am,' Rusty declared hotly. 'Bullying lily-livered townsmen? Burning nesters' miserable sod huts? That's not man's work. That's work for rats!'

'Then why did you stay?'

Rusty shrugged helplessly. 'We took Bricklin's money.'

It was answer enough.

'Have you known this man long?' Hunter inquired curiously.

'Cole? Hell yes. We've covered a lot of country together, him an' me. He's always treated me right. Now I guess it's payback time.'

Rusty suddenly looked surprised, as though a thought had struck him. Then he turned and glared at Hunter. 'It was you doin' the shootin' back there, wasn't it, Marshal!' he grated. 'It was you shot Cole!'

'That's right,' Hunter replied coolly. 'And the others. But I didn't shoot you while you were dragging Cole to safety, did I?'

'No, I guess you didn't. Why not?'

'Because I reckon any man who'd risk his life to save another is too good a man to kill. As the Good Book says, "Greater love hath no man than he who lays down his life for his friend".'

A silence fell. Rusty stared at Hunter, taking in his black suit and hat and the well-worn gunbelt round his waist. Then his eyes widened with understanding.

'I guess you must be the preacher,' he said slowly. 'I've heard of you!'

'Nothing bad, I hope!' Hunter replied sardonically.

'That depends what side you're on,' the gunman said with a chuckle. 'Old Man Bricklin sure hates yer guts.'

'"He that pursueth evil, pursueth it to his death",' the preacher replied with a shrug.

'*Proverbs*, Chapter 11. Verse 19.'

Rusty looked embarrassed. He wasn't used to men quoting the Bible at him. 'Maybe so,' he said doubtfully, 'but he says he'll pay a thousand dollars to the man that kills you. And he's hired another ten men on top of the thirty he had on the payroll already.'

'What about you?' the preacher probed. 'You aiming to try for the money later on?'

The gunman bridled angrily. 'No I ain't!' he flared. 'I'm done with Bricklin.' His anger died as quickly as it had arisen. 'Anyways, I owes you my life, preacher. An' I won't ferget it neither. You could have killed me easy out there.'

'I only kill men who deserve killing,' the preacher said seriously. 'You didn't. But I trust you'll try to make better use of your life from now on. Stop being a hired gun, for example.'

Rusty's eyebrows shot up. 'You tryin' to convert me, preacher?' he said derisively.

'Of course. That's my job, saving brands from the burning,' the preacher replied with a smile. 'What *can* you do apart from slinging a gun?'

'You're serious, ain't you!' The gunman rubbed his chin thoughtfully. 'Well … to tell

183

you true, marshal, I was a wheelwright afore Cole and me went on the dodge. He was a barber. We was fed up to the back teeth with livin' in a small town in Missouri where nuffin' ever happened from one month's end to the next. We wanted adventure while we was still young enuff to enjoy it. So one day we told our bosses what they could do with their jobs and rode out, headin' West.'

He sighed gustily, 'We was only lookin' fer a bit o' excitement. But we got in with the wrong crowd, I guess. We bin sellin' our guns fer more'n ten years now.'

'Are you any good at it?'

'I earn my pay,' Rusty replied with a faint lift of the shoulders. 'Cole was better than me though.'

He glanced worriedly over at his friend. 'God knows whether he'll ever be able to use a gun again though. You sure made a mess of his shoulder, marshal!'

'That's the risk you run, in your profession,' the preacher said blandly. 'Why don't you give it up?'

'And do what?' the gunman said sourly.

'Settle down somewhere. Get a proper job.' Hunter's eyes twinkled with humour. 'Now that you ask me, Antelope Wells *does* need a wheelwright. A barber too, come to that.'

Rusty's jaw dropped. Was the marshal serious? Could he and his friend really make a new start in Antelope Wells? And if it was a real offer, did he want to take it? The debate was still going on inside his head when the little cavalcade reached the outskirts of Antelope Wells.

Before leaving town the preacher had given the townsmen his instructions. For the last three hours they had been busy. Two heavy wagons partly blocked the road into town. The gap between them was just big enough for one horse at a time to pass through.

Two men were guarding the gap. They were armed to the teeth. They greeted the preacher effusively, relieved to see him back and in one piece. They had heard the shooting over the other side of the river and had feared the worst.

They eyed Rusty and his wounded friend curiously as Hunter led them into the town, but something in the marshal's eye stopped them from asking him any questions about the two men.

Looking up as they rode along, Rusty saw armed men on the roof-tops. Every man they came across was carrying a gun of some sort and they all looked determined to fight to the death in defence of their little town.

Rusty decided that his former companions were going to get a hell of a shock if they came riding into Antelope Wells. Not so long ago they had swaggered through the town like conquerors. They had threatened and browbeaten the men and insulted the women.

Bill Lonegan had tried to stand up to them, but that had only got him killed. Then some of the townsmen had pulled up stakes and moved away. The remaining townspeople had cowered before the gunmen whenever they rode into town.

But things were different now. The preacher had turned these rabbits into wolves.

Harry Rose was sitting in a rocker on the stoop outside his shop when Hunter and his prisoners rode slowly towards him. An old Dance revolver left over from the Civil War was shoved through his waistband and a battered Henry rifle was leaning against the wall behind him. He eyed the two strangers speculatively for a moment, noting the blood caked on the one man's shirt and the other man's empty holster and rifle boot.

'You sure sent Bricklin's men runnin' home with a flea in their ears, marshal,' he called admiringly. 'How many of 'em did you kill, out there?'

'Three,' Hunter replied. Rosey had the reputation of being the biggest gossip in town, not excluding the womenfolk. Tell him and the whole town would know pretty quick. The news of his success out there would further encourage the townspeople to resist Deke Bricklin and his men.

'And these two?'

'My prisoners. Is Doc Thompson at home?'

'Naw. He's in the saloon. D'you want me to get him for you?'

'I'd be obliged if you would.'

'Sure thing, marshal.'

The preacher nodded his thanks and the three horses walked on down the street. Behind them Rosey jumped to his feet and set off to fetch Doc Thompson.

The preacher was pleased by what he saw as they rode up the street. The town was an armed camp. The other end of the street was blocked with two more wagons and guarded by a couple of heavily armed men.

There were men on the roof-tops and armed men lounging in doorways. Some of them looked uncomfortable with their unaccustomed pistols and rifles, but they all look determined to sell their lives dearly.

Hunter led the two men to Doc Thompson's house. He dismounted and, at a nod from Hunter, Rusty did the same. Between them they lifted Cole from his saddle. Although the movement must have hurt the wounded gunman he made no sound. He had fainted from loss of blood. It was a tribute to his strong body that he was still alive.

One of the saloon loafers came ambling up to see what was going on. He was carrying an old Volcanic repeating carbine.

'That's Cole Morris!' he yelped. 'He rides for Deke Bricklin! Why're you bringin' him in to the doc's?'

'Because he's wounded, of course,' Hunter said contemptuously.

'Who the hell cares what happens to scum like that?' the unshaven saloon loafer said roughly. 'Let him bleed to death, why don't you? It'll save the town the trouble of a hanging.'

Rusty's face fell. What was all this talk of hanging? He turned to the preacher. 'You said we'd be safe!'

The preacher smiled reassuringly. 'And so you shall. This man has no influence here.'

The loafer scowled blackly. He had been drinking steadily all morning and the whiskey had made him reckless.

'I ain't a gun fighter like you or Bricklin's men,' he sneered, 'but I guess I can use a gun when I have to. And when I'm shootin' Bricklin's men in their fronts I sure as hell don't want these men shootin' me in the back!'

The preacher's cold grey eyes bored into the loafer's bloodshot orbs. 'You talk a good fight, Sykes.' His voice was heavy with scorn. 'I hope you'll do as well when Bricklin and his men arrive. I shall be watching, to see how you get on. As for these two men, they have broken with Bricklin.'

'But...' the loafer protested.

'But nothing!' Hunter cut him off and there was a snap in his voice that promised trouble if the man persisted. 'Get back to your post, Sykes.'

Mumbling a surly apology Sykes turned away.

Doc Thompson came waddling up. A Greener shotgun dangled from his hand. He took one look at the wounded man and said, 'Bring him inside.'

Hunter and Rusty carried Cole into the doctor's surgery and laid him down on the operating table. The doctor propped his shotgun against the wall, stripped off his coat and rolled up his sleeves. Then while he washed his hands and spread out his instruments the preacher began to unfasten the wounded man's blood-soaked shirt.

Cole Morris was a burly man with a broad well-muscled chest. Hunter's bullet had hit him just below the junction of the shoulder joint and collar-bone. Blood was still welling from the hole in a sluggish stream. Looking down into the wound Hunter could see the white of splintered bone.

'Now hold him down, both of you,' said Doc Thompson and while Rusty and Hunter looked on apprehensively he began to probe the wound with a pair of forceps. Somewhere in that mass of torn flesh and shattered bone was a .44 slug and some shreds of Cole's shirt and undershirt. It all had to come out if the man were to have a chance of survival.

Twenty minutes later Hunter and Rusty came out of the doctor's house and flopped down on a bench. The operation had gone well. Doc Thompson had removed the bullet from the gunman's smashed shoulder and repaired the damage as best he could.

Cole had recovered consciousness half-way through the operation and it had taken all the two men's strength to hold him still while Doc prodded and probed at the wound. Digging for the flattened lump of lead had been a messy business. By the time Doc had finished his work and Cole had relapsed into unconsciousness again both men were plain tuckered out.

The preacher rolled himself a smoke and passed the makings to Rusty. They were enjoying a companionable smoke when John Chapman came hurrying across the street from his store. The six nesters were with him.

'Marshal?' said Chapman, who seemed to have been elected as spokesman for the nesters.

'Yes, what is it?'

'My friends here want to know what has happened to their homes.'

'Bricklin's men only got to burn one house,' Hunter began reassuringly. 'That was yours, I'm afraid, Mr Prynne.'

The young farmer shrugged wryly. 'That's no surprise. It was the first one they come to.'

'We'll all help you build it again, good as new, won't we, boys?' Jake Morrison said sympathetically, and the other men promptly agreed. 'It won't take long, not if we all work together.'

'Thank you, all of you,' Prynne said gratefully.

'The town will help you too,' the store-keeper asserted.

'I appreciates that, Mr Chapman. I really do.' The nester smiled gratefully at his friends, old and new.

The storekeeper turned back to face Hunter. 'We thought we heard a deal of shooting out there,' he said questioningly.

'I would have thought Rosey'd have told you all about it by now,' Hunter replied with a smile.

Chapman grinned. He was well aware that Rosey was a grade A gossip. The six nesters, who didn't, looked blank.

'Bricklin is short of five men. Three of them are still out there. One is in Doc Thompson's hands, he isn't going anywhere for a while, and Rusty here has seen the error of his ways.'

The preacher gestured lazily with his cigarette. 'That's right, isn't it, Rusty?'

The red-headed gunman smiled wryly. 'Sure is, marshal. I'm a *reee*formed character.'

John Chapman looked sceptically at Rusty's empty holster. 'Is that so? I see the marshal doesn't trust you with a gun though.'

Hunter took Rusty's Frontier Colt from

his waistband and hefted it in his hand for a moment.

'Thanks for reminding me, John,' he said blandly. He tossed the gun to Rusty. 'Here! Catch!'

The red-headed gunman snatched the gun out of the air and slipped it into his holster. He put out his hand. The preacher stretched across and gripped it firmly.

'I won't let you down, marshal,' Rusty said in a voice that was choked with emotion. 'And I'll go bail for Cole too, when he's all healed up.'

The preacher got to his feet. 'I don't know about you, Rusty,' he said casually. 'But I'm pretty hungry. Do you want to come down to the diner and get some grub?'

'Sure thing,' replied Rusty, and got to his feet, settling his gunbelt comfortably round his narrow hips.

'See you later, boys,' said Hunter, and tipping his hat to the storekeeper and the nesters, he and Rusty strode off down the street towards Ma Considine's diner.

ELEVEN

Later that day the lookout on the top of the hotel saw a plume of dust heading their way and gave the alarm. Men rushed out of their houses, hurriedly buckling on their guns, and took up their assigned positions. They cocked their guns and waited nervously for something to happen.

Bricklin's men reined in just out of rifle range. The two heavy wagons blocked the main street and prevented them from riding into town in a body.

They hadn't expected that. It took them a couple of minutes to decide what to do. The watching townspeople saw the massive figure of Deke Bricklin waving his arms as he gave his orders.

The gunmen split into two groups. One rode down the left-hand side of the town, looking for a way in, the other took the right. But all the alleys between the buildings had been blocked with heavy timbers or piles of chairs and tables. Everywhere they looked they saw rifles and shotgun

195

barrels point at them.

When the two parties of gunmen reached the far end of town they discovered that the end of the street was blocked by a second pair of wagons.

By now Bricklin and his men were losing their tempers and there was another heated discussion. Eventually a small band of gunmen split off from the main body and rode back towards the far end of town. The rest of them led by their red-faced and furious boss drew their guns, kicked their horses into a gallop and charged the barrier.

Deke Bricklin had more than thirty men with him. It was the biggest cavalry charge anyone in town had seen since the end of the War.

The rancher was sure that most of the townspeople hadn't got the guts to fight him. He'd have to kill the marshal, of course, and maybe a few others, but after that the people of Antelope Wells would throw down their guns and run like rabbits.

When Bricklin and his men got into range they sent a blizzard of lead heading towards the barrier. Bullets thumped into the thick oak planks of the wagons and whizzed alarmingly over the heads of the cowering defenders. They were about to turn and run when Hunter came running up to help them.

'Make every shot count.' Hunter's voice was calm but it stiffened the men's backbones amazingly. 'Ready. Aim. Fire!'

Each of the men lining the barrier chose a target and squeezed off a shot. The men on the tops of the nearby buildings fired their weapons a split second later.

Because they were nervous their aim was bad and only two of the riders were hit. One man took a bullet in the head. He slumped sideways and fell off his horse. His left foot caught in the stirrups and he was dragged along in a cloud of dust. The other man was hit in the side. He swayed in the saddle but kept his seat cursing loudly, retreated out of range at top speed.

Hunter rested his pistol on the side of the wagon and took careful aim at Deke Bricklin. With him dead his men would lose much of their enthusiasm for the fight. But as the hammer came down on the shell one of the rancher's hired guns rode between them and took the bullet in his throat. He fell off his horse, spouting blood.

Before the preacher could fire again the rancher had turned his horse and vanished into the surging crowd of gunmen.

The ways of the Lord are passing strange, thought the preacher, then turned his gun on another of Bricklin's men, a wiry young man with a cast in one eye. The .44 barked and the man sprouted a third eye between and just above the other two, fell forward over his saddle horn, and slumped bone-lessly to the ground.

Bricklin's men rode up and down the barrier firing at anyone they could see. The men behind the wagons fired back. The clouds of choking grey smoke from the roaring guns soon mingled with the billowing dust thrown up by the churning hooves to make a fog through which neither side could see their enemies clearly.

Both sides kept on firing into the smoke, hoping to make a lucky hit. A couple of Bricklin's men were wounded, though not seriously, and one of the defenders was killed outright, but for the moment neither side seemed to have the advantage.

In a lull in the firing the preacher heard the sound of gunfire coming from the other end of the street. It seemed that more of Bricklin's men were attacking the barrier down there. Maybe he ought to get down there and stiffen the defence.

He took a quick glance at the men beside

him. Their faces were blackened with powdersmoke but they had big grins on their faces. They had stood up to Bricklin and his hired guns and made them back off. They had recovered their pride.

Rio Harkness guessed what Hunter was thinking. 'Go on, marshal,' he urged. 'You ain't needed here. We can hold 'em off till doomsday, can't we, boys?'

'Sure can!'

To Hunter's surprise, Jem Sykes was the speaker. But he was a different man now from the one who'd suggested lynching Rusty and his friend Cole only a short while before. He stood proudly, gun in hand, secure in the knowledge that he was doing his bit. He had regained his self-respect.

The other man promptly declared that from behind these wagons they could hold off an army. The preacher gratefully accepted their assurances and ran off down the street in the direction of the sound of gunfire.

This was a bad mistake.

Shortly after he left the barrier Bricklin's men attacked it again. This time they had a plan. Under the cover of the rolling clouds of gunsmoke two gunmen crept up to the barrier and tied their lariats to the pole of one of the wagons. Then they handed the other ends of the braided leather ropes to a couple of their companions, who fastened them to their saddlehorns and backed their horses away from the mêlée.

The wagon creaked as the ropes went taut, then began to move.

The men hiding behind the wagon ran for the shelter of a nearby barn. Two of them never reached it. They were shot down as they ran. Rio Harkness and three more dived through the open door of the building and rolled out of sight.

The way into Antelope Wells was wide open.

Deke Bricklin stood up in his stirrups and waved his hat over his head. 'Come on, boys!' he yelled. 'We've got 'em now!' He dug his spurs into his horse's sides and the animal leapt forward, carrying him through the gap in the town's defences and into the main street of Antelope Wells. His men raced after their boss, guns at the ready.

Jem Sykes had been too proud to run away with the others. He threw himself under the nearest wagon and levered shot after shot at the gunmen from his old Spencer carbine. Most of them missed their targets, but the last bullet in the magazine hit a gunman square between the shoulder-blades, and, passing through his chest, blew his heart to rags. The man threw up his arms and fell off his horse.

Ben Strutt wheeled his horse and rode back to the barrier. Jem Sykes was feverishly thumbing bullets into his weapon. He heard the approaching hoofbeats and looked up to see Ben Strutt looming over him.

'Goodbye, sucker.' The saturnine gunman brought his pistol into line, his finger tightened on the trigger, the pistol spat flame and the bullet smashed into the townsman's face and burst out of the back of his head in a shower of blood and brains.

Deke Bricklin and his men rode up and down the main street of Antelope Wells firing at everyone they saw. Dust rose up in choking clouds from under their horses' hooves. Bullets smashed windows and splintered doors and walls.

The townsmen fired back from their windows and roofs. Few of them were better than average with a gun, but there was so much lead flying about that they were bound to make hits sooner or later. And Bricklin's men were out in the street without any shelter while the townsmen were hidden behind walls. That evened out the odds to some extent.

The town was suffering a good deal of damage. All the buildings were made of wood and presented little obstacle to a bullet. Soon every wall and door was pocked with bullet holes and every pane of glass had been smashed.

A stray bullet shattered the mirror behind the bar of the Castle saloon. Curly Watts had brought that mirror all the way over the plains from St Louis. Furious at the loss of his most cherished possession he flung himself through the batwing doors of the saloon and loosed off his shotgun into the crowd of riders. The two loads of buckshot blasted one man to doll rags and badly wounded another.

That'll teach those bastards to smash my mirror, he thought delightedly and hurriedly ducked back into the building as a stream of hot lead whizzed over his head.

Further down the street the storekeeper was having himself a good time. He was the local agent for the Winchester Rifle Company and had ten of their latest model .44-40 carbine in stock. He had taken them all upstairs and was shooting from a window overlooking the street.

He was only a fair to middling shot, but a

Winchester holds sixteen .44-40 shells and was working the lever as fast as he could go. When he emptied one rifle his wife Mary handed him another and began thumbing shells into the empty one.

As the town's gunsmith, Theodore Dardick had to repair all sorts of guns, from Jim Bacher's old Hawken muzzle-loading rifle to the latest Colts and Remingtons, and test them too. He was probably the town's best shot.

His wife was pregnant and near her time. She had begged him to stay home and guard her, but he had told her firmly that the best way of keeping her safe was to kill as many of Bricklin's men as possible.

Now he was up on the roof of the hotel with a Sharps buffalo gun, picking off gunman after gunman, cool as you like. And anyone hit by the thumb-sized bullet from his Sharps Big .50 wasn't *ever* getting up again.

The nesters were making good their brag of all being ex-army men. Their single-shot Ballards and Springfields fired more slowly than the repeaters the townsmen were using but they hit their targets more often and the men they hit stayed hit.

Down at the other end of town the

preacher joined Obadiah Somers, Jim Bacher, Rusty Timms, and a couple of the nesters at the barricade just as ten of Bricklin's men attacked their position.

Instead of riding round and round, firing at the defenders, the gunmen rode straight up to the barrier and leaped from their saddles on to the wagons, their guns blazing.

The defenders were caught completely by surprise. Obadiah Somers caught a bullet in the brisket and went down, leaking blood. One of the nesters had his arm broken by a bullet. Fortunately it was his right arm and he was left-handed and still able to shoot.

Jim Bacher knocked one man off his horse with his old Hawken rifle as they rode up, but he was no hand with a short gun. If it hadn't been for Rusty Timms, who fanned his gun and killed three of his former comrades, forcing the rest of them to back up a mite, the gunmen would have broken through the town's defences on this side.

Then Hunter arrived. His first shot, fired on the run, knocked one man backwards off the wagon into the dirt. His second hit a burly unshaven ruffian in the belly and doubled him up, screaming thinly. The third bullet went through a redshirted gunman's open mouth and blew the back of his head off.

The remaining gunmen scrambled down from the wagon, ran to their horses, mounted up and galloped away. Once they were out of pistol-shot they headed back towards the far end of the town to join the rest of the attacking party.

Jim Bacher reloaded his old muzzle-loading rifle with the deftness of long practice. He took a percussion cap out of his waistcoat pocket and fitted it carefully over the nipple. Then he eared back the hammer and snuggled the ancient weapon into his shoulder.

One of the retreating gunmen wore a black-and-white cowhide vest. Bacher took aim between the man's broad shoulders, held his breath for a moment, and gently squeezed the trigger. The hammer swept down, striking the percussion cap and firing the charge of black powder in the barrel. The rifle coughed smoke and a round lead ball thumped into the man's back with deadly force. He toppled sideways off his horse. His cowardly companions made no effort to help him, but crouched low over their saddles and urged their mounts to even greater speed.

Jim Bacher lowered his smoking rifle and grinned at Hunter. 'I *told* you ol' Betsy was a straight-shootin' gun, didn't I, marshal!' he cackled.

'So you did,' the preacher agreed gravely.

A sudden burst of firing from behind him made his head snap round. Looking down the street he saw Deke Bricklin and his men pour through a gap in the barrier and ride into the town.

The preacher realized that he had made a big mistake by leaving his post at the other barrier and started to run back the way he had come.

The angry gunmen seemed determined to do as much damage as they could. They galloped round and round in the centre of the street pouring lead into every door and window within sight.

Deke Bricklin saw the black-clad marshal running down the street and forgot all about his vendetta against the town. This man had killed his son!

The rancher jabbed his spurs into his horse's sides and as the huge red stallion leapt forward his men hurriedly wheeled their horses aside to let him pass.

Hunter saw Bricklin coming and slid to a halt, raising his Colt .44.

The rancher's gun was already in his hand. It suddenly bloomed flame and smoke and a bullet whistled past Hunter's head. That was good shooting from the top deck of a galloping horse. The rancher was much closer now. He fired again and Hunter felt a smashing blow on his hip. He staggered and fell, rolling on to his left side as he hit the ground.

Hunter pointed his gun at the charging rancher and squeezed the trigger. The spinning lump of lead went in under Bricklin's jaw and smashed its way out through the top of his head. The rancher was dead at last, and all his pent up hatred and fury with him.

The great red stallion pounded down the street with Deke Bricklin sitting bolt upright but stone dead in the saddle until it came to the barrier. Then it dug in its hooves and came to a sliding stop with its haunches almost touching the ground.

The rancher's body was catapulted over his horse's head and landed on top of one of the wagons, where it hung, head down, leaking blood and brains all over the woodwork.

Their employer's sudden and dramatic death knocked all the fight out of the remaining gunmen. Led by Ben Strutt they wheeled their horses and rode full pelt for the end of town and the trail that led to the D-B Connected.

Ben Strutt was a quick thinker. Now Deke Bricklin and his son were dead the D-B Connected was up for grabs, and he was the logical candidate to take over.

Maybe the preacher had inspired the townspeople to stand up to Bricklin's attempt to take over the town, but he sure as hell wouldn't be able to persuade them to form a posse to chase him and the surviving gunmen out of the valley. The townsmen valued their own skins too highly for that.

He knew that none of the other gunmen would have the guts to challenge his ownership of the D-B Connected. They weren't good enough with a gun. But they were plenty good enough for what he wanted them to do. And that was go after the other ranchers, one by one.

That had been Deke Bricklin's mistake, the scarfaced gunman thought smugly. If Bricklin had driven out the other ranchers before threatening Antelope Wells he probably wouldn't have needed to attack the town at all. It would have fallen into his hands like a ripe plum.

The preacher slowly got to his feet. His hip was a mass of pain. He looked down, wondering just what he would see there. It sure felt like a major wound.

To his surprise there was no blood on his hip, though his gunbelt was all blackened and torn and his tailored pants were scorched and burnt. The rancher's bullet had hit his gunbelt just below his hip-bone and exploded a couple of shells in their loops. From the feel of things he would have a mighty big bruise there tomorrow.

But it could have been so much worse, he thought, and as he limped up the street he offered the Lord God his silent and grateful thanks for saving him once again from the efforts of the ungodly.

As the gunmen beat a speedy retreat three more of them fell victim to the townsmen's fury.

Dardick popped up from his place on the hotel roof and shot one man off his horse with his Sharps Big .50. The massive slug blew a hole in the man's thigh that was big enough to put a fist in and ploughed on through flesh and bone to kill the horse he was riding stone dead. Horse and man collapsed together in a bloody heap.

John Chapman got another man, much to

his surprise. He had already used up most of a box of .44-40 shells without hitting anyone, though he had wounded a couple of horses and thrown quite a scare into Rosey and Doc Thompson, who were firing their own weapons from across the street. They found his wild bullets whistling past their heads and thumping into the woodwork mighty disconcerting.

Now the gunmen were no longer shooting back at him the storekeeper stopped working the lever of his Winchester like a pump handle and took the time to aim properly before gently squeezing off a shot.

The last of the gunmen jerked suddenly as the storekeeper's bullet hit him, then he slid gently off his horse.

John Chapman's mouth fell open with an almost audible clang. His wife Mary threw her arms round her husband. 'You got him! You got him,' she cried and kissed her husband soundly.

Chapman kissed her back, hard. They had won, he was still alive, and he had done his share. His wife had seen him do it too. That was as much as any man could hope for.

As the band of gunmen thundered down the street in a hail of bullets from the triumphant townsmen Rio Harkness stepped out of the barn where he and the other men from the broken barricade had been sheltering. He had seen Ben Strutt murder Jem Sykes and burned to avenge him.

His first bullet whipped Strutt's hat from his head and his second missed the cold-hearted gunman by a whisker and killed the man riding close behind him.

Despite the fact that he was firing from horseback Ben Strutt made no mistake with his own shot. The bullet hit Rio just below the Bull Durham tag hanging from his vest pocket and smashed his heart into bloody rags. The pistol fell from the cowboy's nerveless fingers and he slumped to the ground, dead as a herring.

Ben Strutt aimed his horse for the gap between the two wagons at the end of the street. Once through the gap they would be safe.

Suddenly the end of the street was full of strange riders. They all had guns in their hands. The guns spouted flame and a torrent of shot smashed into the hapless band of gunmen. Half of them were either killed or wounded in that first volley.

The surviving gunmen hauled on their reins and swung their horses away from the rolling thunder of the guns. The strange riders came after them, firing as they came, and there were more men pressing into the gap behind them.

There was nowhere for Ben Strutt and his men to go. They milled about in the centre of the street as hot lead tore into them from every side. Man after man fell from their saddles, wounded or dead.

Ben Strutt's horse was hit by a stray bullet. It staggered, coughing blood, and collapsed. As it fell to the dusty street and rolled over on to its side, legs kicking spasmodically, the gunman freed his feet from the stirrups and sprang aside.

Just then the preacher came limping up the street.

'Drop your gun, Strutt,' he called. 'You can see it's all over!'

Ben Strutt knew that already. Most of his men were dead. But he had nothing to gain by surrendering. The people of Antelope Wells wanted him hanged for killing Bill Lonegan.

Well, he thought bitterly, if he was going to die he might as well go out in style. The preacher's gun was in his holster. His own gun was in his hand. He could easily put a couple of bullets in his black-clad nemesis before the townsmen cut him down.

He would be remembered throughout the West as the man who shot the preacher. That was an epitaph worth dying for!

Ben Strutt's hand moved with the quickness of a striking snake. His pearl-handled Remington came up and pointed at the preacher. He pulled the trigger. The gun cracked and a tongue of flame licked out towards his opponent. He never got a chance to fire a second shot.

Hunter's gun was already out of its holster and coming up into line as Ben Strutt fired, and although he staggered as the bullet thumped into his chest his gun stayed as steady as a rock. His index finger held the trigger down as his left hand swept across the hammer again and again.

Few men ever mastered the art of fanning a pistol. In inexperienced hands it was almost guaranteed to spray bullets all over the surrounding landscape while missing the target entirely. But Hunter was an expert.

Ben Strutt was hit by six lead slugs in the space of less than two seconds. Three hit him in the belly, cutting it wide open. Two more hit him in the chest, dyeing his shirt red with blood. The last slug smashed his teeth and tore his tongue to rags before exiting through the back of his neck.

The scar-faced gunman fell to the ground like a puppet whose strings had been cut. Blood poured from his wounds and soaked away into the dust.

The preacher slipped his hand into his coat and ran it over his chest, feeling for the stickiness of blood. He had felt Ben Strutt's bullet smash into his ribs but for some reason there was no pain. Not yet, anyway.

His questing fingers found nothing. His vest and shirt were quite dry and untorn. He took his Bible from the inside pocket of his coat and stared at it in disbelief. The front cover was torn and holed. He opened the book and saw that the bullet from Ben Strutt's gun had bored a ragged hole almost all the way through the thick volume. When he opened the back cover a misshapen lead slug fell into his palm. It was still warm.

Ignoring the gunfight going on all round him Hunter briefly shut his eyes and whispered a silent prayer of thanks to the Almighty, who had saved him once again.

Ben Strutt's death took all the stuffing out of the remaining gunmen. One of them suddenly dropped his gun and raised his hands into the air. Another followed, then another and another.

The preacher threw his arms in the air and yelled: 'Cease firing! Cease firing!'

The sudden silence that followed his command was deafening.

The townsmen could hardly believe it was all over. Very cautiously they began to come out of their houses and shops. Their womenfolk hung back warily, wanting to be sure it was quite safe before following their men on to the sidewalks.

Some of the townsmen had minor bullet wounds, others were dripping blood from cuts caused by flying glass from windows broken by the gunmen's bullets, but apart from Jem Sykes, Rio Harkness and two other men killed when the barrier of wagons gave way, plus Obadiah Somers, shot down defending the other end of town, no one else had been seriously hurt.

The gunmen had been far less fortunate. The dead and wounded littered the street. Pools of blood lay everywhere. Wounded men cried for help or called for their mothers.

Deke Bricklin had brought nearly forty men to attack Antelope Wells. Less than a dozen of them were alive and unwounded. They sat their horses in the centre of the street with their hands in the air, looking sullen and apprehensive.

More than likely all they had bought by their surrender was a quick trial with a necktie party to follow. But at least that was better than being shot to doll rags like their former companions.

The leader of the band of riders who had prevented the gunmen's escape bid and in doing so saved Antelope Valley from a great deal of future trouble and strife rode forward to meet the preacher. His eyes were twinkling. His lips curved in a smile behind his bristling white moustache.

'Bet you never thought you'd see *us* riding to your rescue, marshal,' he chuckled.

The preacher touched his hat. 'Mighty obliged, Mr Teale,' he said with a smile. 'The same goes for all you men. Antelope Wells is grateful for your assistance.'

John Chapman stepped forward, his Winchester dangling from his hand. 'The marshal's right, isn't he boys!' he called. 'Let's give Mr Teale and his men a cheer!'

The townsmen's throats were hoarse from breathing powdersmoke and yelling to each other over the crash of gunfire, but their cheers still managed to raise the roof.

John Chapman turned to the preacher and shook his hand firmly. 'And now, let's show our appreciation of the man who led us to victory over Bricklin and his bully-boys! One, two, three…!'

This time the cheer that came from the throats of the triumphant townsfolk must have been heard all the way to the county seat!

The preacher shrugged dismissively. 'I only pointed the way,' he said. 'You men did all the real work. And don't forget God Almighty. He has fought hard for us today.'

Doc Thompson came out of his office, his shotgun dangling forgotten from his hand. Now the fighting was over his first concern was for the wounded.

'Can we take the wounded into the hotel, Troy?' he asked, then without waiting for the hotel-keeper to answer, went on: 'Mrs Rossiter, I'd be obliged if you'd find us some nurses from amongst the womenfolk. You men start carrying the wounded into the hotel. I'll get my things and join you there.'

He stumped off towards the office, leaving the others silently staring after him.

John Chapman was the first to speak. 'You heard the man,' he said with a shrug. 'The fighting's over now. It's time to start clearing up. Some of you drag the deaders down to Jim's place for boxing up, the rest of you help me tote these wounded fellas into the hotel.'

The townsmen shook themselves as if awaking from a dream. It was all over, and they had survived. Suddenly all the excitement had gone away. There were jobs to be done. Soon the street was a hive of activity as the dead men were dragged away and the wounded carried into the hotel for treatment.

John Chapman came up to Hunter. 'What shall we do with these men?' he asked, indicating the group of surviving gunmen.

'You've got two choices,' the preacher replied evenly. 'Hang them, or let them go.'

The storekeeper ran his eyes over the beaten gunmen. Some of them stared back stonily. Others looked scared.

Chapman shrugged. 'I've never been keen on hanging men in cold blood,' he said soberly. 'What do you say we let them go?'

The dozen or so surviving gunmen perked up at that, as well they might.

'That's fine by me,' Hunter replied with a smile. 'God loves a merciful man.'

He raised his voice. 'Mr Teale! Would you send some of your men to escort these men out of the valley?'

'Sure thing,' the white-moustached rancher

agreed, and shortly afterwards the sullen gunmen departed Antelope Wells under escort and with their tails between their legs, having discovered that, given leadership, even the despised townsmen and nesters could give a good account of themselves when the guns started roaring.

A huge cheer went up when Chapman, Teale and Hunter joined the celebrating townsmen, cowboys and nesters in the Castle Saloon.

The preacher was pleased to see that the three groups had completely forgotten their former differences and were drinking side by side in friendship and amity. One of his aims had been to reconcile the ranchers and the nesters. Clearly that had been achieved. Now to set the town on a sound footing.

He held up his hands and called for silence. Slowly the laughter and conversation died away.

'Now that the fighting's over I shall be leaving Antelope Wells,' he began.

A storm of protests promptly broke over his head.

Hunter waited for the cries of dismay to die down, then continued: 'I have to go. There are other places needing my help. But before I go I want to get a few things settled.'

He turned to Benjamin Teale and the other ranchers. 'I take it you men are willing to be friends with the farmers.'

It was not a question.

Teale glanced at his fellow ranchers. They all nodded. Teale put out his hand and Jake Morrison shook it firmly while the other nesters looked on with pleasure.

The preacher smiled with satisfaction. 'Secondly. The town will need a new mayor. I propose John Chapman.'

The storekeeper's jaw fell open.

Hunter grinned at him. 'You did more to help me than anyone, John. If you'll take the job I know I'll be leaving Antelope Wells in good hands.'

The appointment was a popular one and was ratified by acclamation.

'Now we have to take a difficult decision,' the preacher went on. 'What shall we do with the D-B Connected? I understand Deke Bricklin left no heirs. That means the land is up for grabs.'

That started a buzz of comment and speculation. Deke Bricklin's spread was the biggest of the seven ranches. It had the best land and the most water. Bricklin had had more than five thousand beeves. If a man could make himself master of the former D-

B Connected he could live like a king.

But which of the ranchers was strong enough to take it? Range wars had been started over less.

Hunter had already thought of all this and had a solution to the problem ready.

'I suggest you divide the land into sections and invite families to come and settle. The price they pay for the land will let you start up a bank, in which you all, townsmen, nesters and cattlemen alike, can be shareholders. More people in the valley will mean more business for the town, and a bigger market for the ranchers. Everyone will benefit.'

This radical suggestion struck the whole room dumb. The townsmen rather liked the idea of selling off the land and starting a bank with the proceeds. Maybe this would start the town growing again?

The ranchers looked doubtfully at each other. Did they really want more nesters in Antelope Valley? But on the other hand, it was better by far than having another big outfit take over Deke Bricklin's ranch and start throwing its weight about.

Again Benjamin Teale spoke for the ranchers.

'That's OK by us.'

'Us too!' John Chapman said enthusiastically. He strode forward and shook Hunter's hand. 'Not only have you saved this town, Mr Hunter, but by making that suggestion you've given us the chance to see it grow into a city!'

He jumped up onto a chair. 'Mr Hunter always said God sent him to help us. Now I believe it. Let us pray that He will continue to help us after he has gone.'

A deep 'Amen' rose from the crowd.

The preacher turned and pushed his way through the crowd to the door. His work in Antelope Wells was done.

While the victorious townspeople celebrated with the farmers and ranchers in the saloon he quietly returned to the hotel and packed up his bedroll, then walked down to the livery stable, saddled his horse and rode out of the town.